KINGDOM OF SPIRITS
BOUND BY DRAGONS BOOK TWO

ALISHA KLAPHEKE

Copyright © 2024 by Alisha Klapheke

All rights reserved.

No part of this book may be reproduced in any form or by any electronic or mechanical means, including information storage and retrieval systems, without written permission from the author, except for the use of brief quotations in a book review.

Cover Art by Franziska at Cover Dungeon

Dust Jacket on Hardcover by Alexandra Curte

Editing by Laura Josephson

❀ Created with Vellum

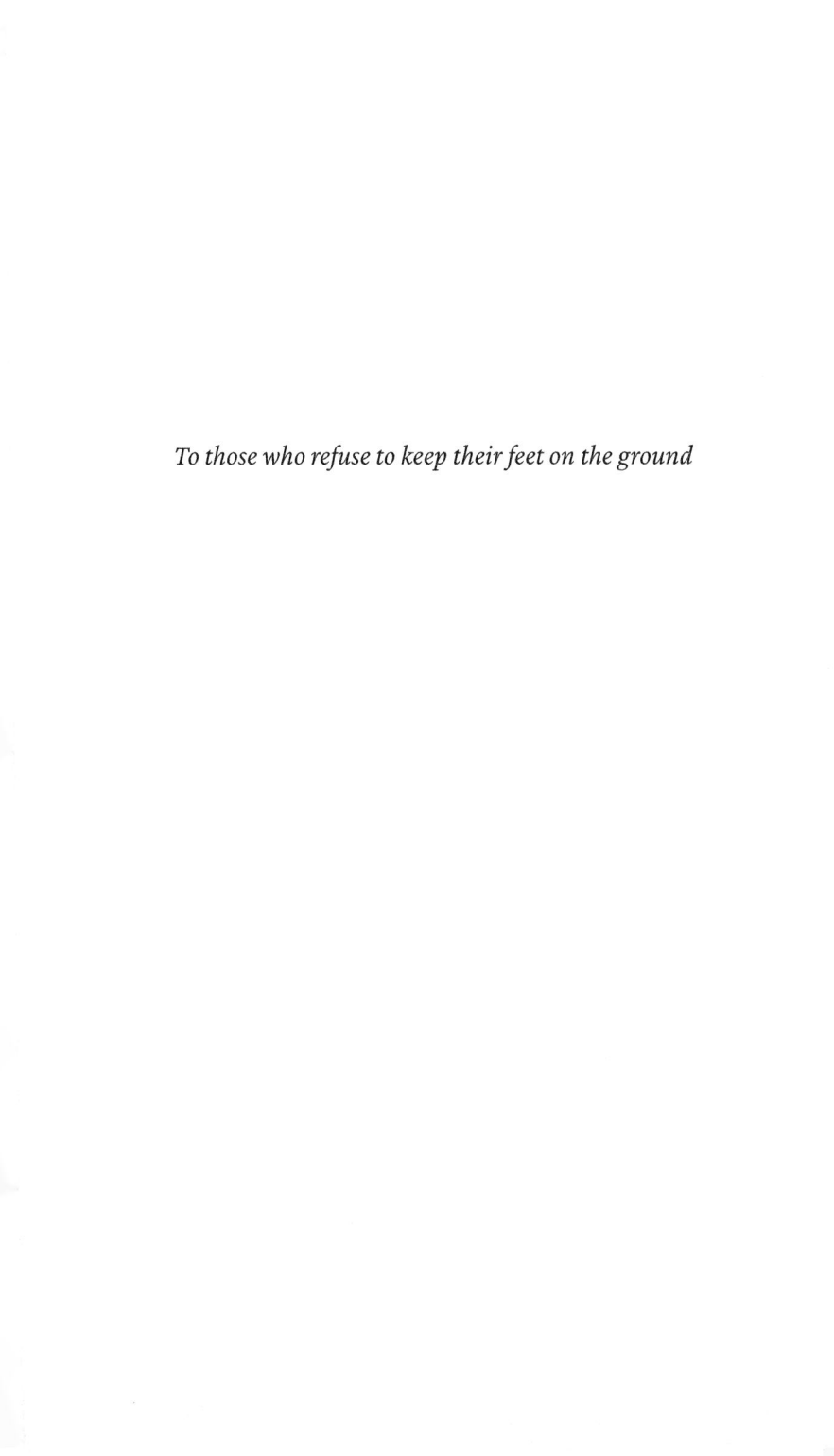

To those who refuse to keep their feet on the ground

SHROUDED MOUNTAINS
REALM OF LIGHTS
Vineyards
Hunting Lodge
Caer Du
Gwerhune
The Fae Forest
FJORDBOK
The Veil
Border River
Veilbury
Midhampton
SAXONION
Isernwyrd
White Sea
Strykeford
DEIGS
Masdam
Glass River
Leptis
LAQQARA
Luxurium
Skull Desert

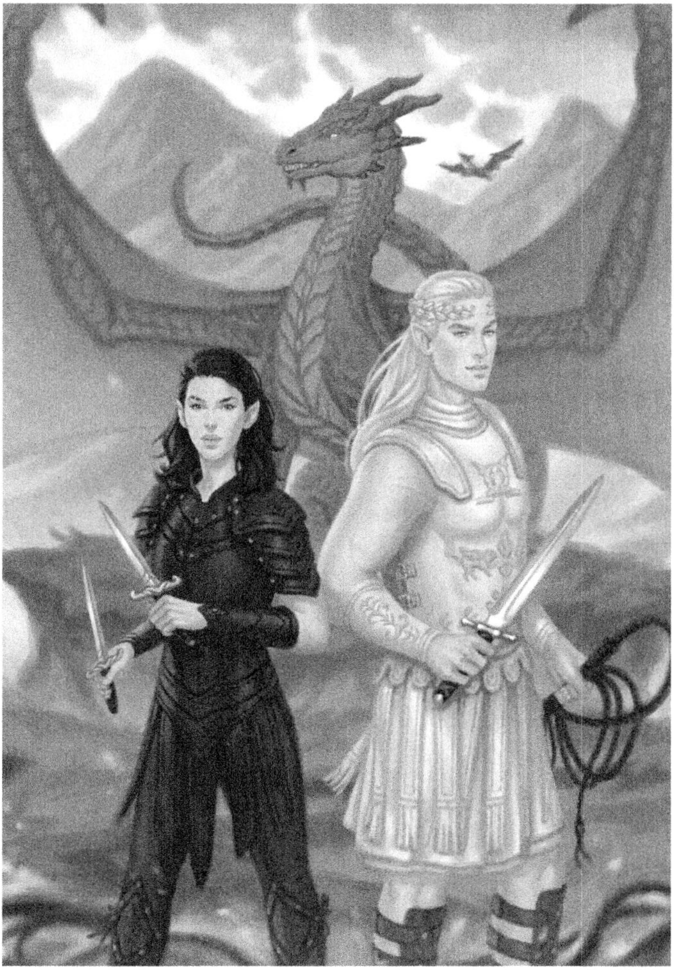

CHAPTER 1
TAHLIA

In the wide expanse of the sunset, wind blasted across Tahlia's face and her braid whipped against her back. Her cyan-hued Seabreak dragon tucked her four dragonfly-like wings and dove through a cloud bank before transitioning into a roll. The dragon's right eye was sore from a scratch received in training yesterday, and an echo of that irritation made Tahlia blink repeatedly. As the dragon completed the roll, Tahlia's stomach tightened, and she whooped, the thrill too much to keep inside. As her dragon zipped by the floating target, Tahlia reached out a hand and smacked the red circle. They had won the day's last training contest. The victory lifted her heart.

"We did it! You're amazing, you know that?" she said, leaning over her dragon's neck and peering through the scattered spikes that defended the creature's spine against attack.

Horns sparkling in the last glow of the day, the Seabreak trilled and blew a puff of smoke. To say that

Tahlia loved the dragon would be a severe understatement. When the dragon had a sore leg, a ghost of that pain echoed in Tahlia's body. In the air, they seemed to share a mind. Tahlia had fallen off a few times during difficult spins and sudden turns, but it was only a lack of physical training that had caused the errors. She had known the Seabreak's coming moves. After more practice, they would be as one, and the dragon wouldn't have to worry about making a dangerous catch with her talons when Tahlia slipped off the saddle.

Titus and his pale blue Spikeback caught up. The Fae male shook a fist and grinned, pretending to be angry that Tahlia had beaten him to the floating target.

Maiwenn and her Seabreak—a male dragon larger than Tahlia's female—soared overhead. Maiwenn's glare wasn't visible at this distance, but still, it burned like a brand.

Ah, well, she'd win Maiwenn over eventually. It had only been fourteen days since Tahlia had earned her place in the Order of the Mist Knights and some of the other dragon riders had yet to truly accept her, mostly because she was half-human.

Tahlia leaned on the dragon's neck. "How about a quick inverted spin?"

With a grunt of approval, the Seabreak spun and flew in a tight coil of movement that had Tahlia holding on with legs and hands both. Her blood sang with the joy of being alive.

"Enough playing around," High Captain Marius Leos Valentius called out, his voice carrying above the wind and the flap of dragon wings.

Tahlia's dragon evened out among the wispy clouds while Tahlia kept staring at Marius.

Gods, he was glorious.

He'd tied back his moon-white hair, showing off his proud nose and jaw. His ears were fully pointed because he was wholly Fae, and his dramatically slitted pupils also spoke to the powerful blood in his veins. He had eyes like a true predator—dangerous, flashing, and altogether impossible to look away from.

And he was hers. Or he would be. They'd had one wild night together, then he'd been called up by the commander to go on a mission for six days. During that time, Tahlia had been thrown to Maiwenn for beginner training. Tahlia already knew a good bit about Marius from the tournament and from the time since he'd returned from his mission, but she wanted to learn everything. And she was more than ready for some one-on-one time with the High Captain.

Biting back a sigh at his beauty, she tapped her dragon's neck and prompted her to land.

All that gorgeous muscle beneath Marius's pale leathers was delectable, and every ounce of that ferocious passion, as well as his lightning-like presence, lured her like the best bait—yes, she had completely fallen for him. Who could blame her?

Tahlia smiled at him and wiggled her eyebrows, knowing his full Fae blood made his vision astoundingly fantastic.

He tilted his head and gave her a good scowl, but she was close enough to see his hand flexing on his reins. It was a tell he had, a movement that meant he was torn between one feeling and another. After hours together in the sky—in the time between her awful training with Maiwenn—she'd seen that particular tick several times.

Her gaze snagged on his hand again and a memory of their night together wrapped around her mind. The heat of that hand of his between her legs. His scent of cloves. The weight of him over her. Whispers of what their future might be...

She shook off those lovely thoughts and prepared for landing, focusing on the job she had to do. The Seabreak spread her four ocean-blue wings wide and caught the wind. They dropped gracefully into the arena. Titus and his Spikeback landed beside them, and then Marius and his Heartsworn dragon alighted in front of the three gathered units of knights.

Marius dismounted his dragon, a handsome scarlet fellow named Ragewing, and he regarded the knights. His gaze barely snagged on Tahlia, but it did indeed snag. She smiled. He might have been quite the stern warrior, but she knew he was falling for her too. Had to be. It was too early to call it anything, but he had stood with her during her struggle to join the knights, and the sparks between them were undeniable.

"Good work up there today, units one and three. Two, you need to keep a tighter line when in the triangle formation. Maiwenn, you still feel up to the position, yes?"

He had named the other Seabreak rider the new captain of unit two after the old captain retired. Maiwenn was a powerful rider, very skilled. Maiwenn and Titus were the best riders after Marius.

Marius served as High Captain of all three units and particularly led unit one, the one Tahlia was in. She was determined to be the best rider in the skies by the end of the summer.

"More training at that level and we will be sure to smoke the northern pirates come autumn," Marius said, almost smiling.

A cheer rose from the knights and Tahlia joined in.

Raising his arms to quiet the gathered knights, Marius said, "Let's celebrate today's training at The Brass Lantern. We can toast our progress with our new recruit." He glanced Tahlia's way, his eyes sparkling with praise that made her stomach flip. "And strengthen our bonds with one another. A tight-knit community is key in times of danger. We must rely on and trust one another despite any differences."

"Aye, High Captain," Titus called out, several echoing him.

Everyone began dismounting and leading their dragons to the water troughs near the public stands of the arena.

"We have to come up with a name for you, darling," Tahlia said to the Seabreak.

The first stars of the early evening glittered across the dragon's ocean-colored scales. Their light cast a veil of silver across her four folded wings, making them sparkle like jewels. As the dragon drank beside Titus's Spikeback, Tahlia splashed water over the Seabreak's head. The dragon eyed her, love shining in the depths of those fire-hued beauties. Tahlia would never stop being amazed that such a massive and dangerous creature could be gentle with her, a tiny half-human, half-Fae female.

Trilling with satisfaction, the Seabreak extended one wing to nudge Tahlia, a show of affection.

"No name yet, hmm?" Titus glanced at Tahlia as he wiped his dragon down with a cloth.

"Nope." And until she and the Seabreak agreed on a name, the bonding wasn't fully formed. Dragon magic was a subtle and prickly thing. Names were as important to them as to their Fae riders. Each dragon had a name that their bonded rider used as well as a name that only belonged to them. How riders knew that second fact was a mystery. Most believed dragons imbued their riders with knowledge through their magic somehow.

"It'll come to you," Titus said. "I have no doubts about your bond." He studied the Seabreak and nodded. "She cares for you already. It's obvious in the way she doesn't shield the underside of her chin from you."

Titus was Marius's second in unit one, the rider who gave orders when Marius was elsewhere or when he was working with another unit. A meaty hunk of a fellow who was quick to laugh, Titus felt like the older brother Tahlia had always wished she'd had. Her real older brother had been borderline abusive. She was glad she'd never lay eyes on him again.

"How about Gertrude?" Tahlia whispered to the Seabreak. The dragon snorted and Tahlia laughed. "Just kidding. Not that. How about Stormwave?" With a growl, the dragon wiggled her snout until Tahlia's arm was slung over the back of the Seabreak's head. "Really? I liked that one. It was Fara's idea." Fara was Tahlia's dearest friend. She served as Tahlia's squire, though she had no plans of working her way into the Order of Mist Knights. "Maybe Coral?" Tahlia suggested. She and the dragon sighed in unison. "Right. Too basic. Well, we will think of something."

"Lady Tahlia." Marius's deep voice startled Tahlia and she spun with fists raised. He lifted an eyebrow at her stance. "That could be construed as an offense to your High Captain, rider."

Tahlia felt light enough to fly without a dragon beneath her. She fought a grin and lowered her arms. "You can't just pop up behind me like that."

Moving toward her, Marius nearly closed the distance between them, and Tahlia looked up at him, craning her neck to do so. The breath of space spreading from his body to hers filled with a simmering tension. He leaned close to whisper in her ear.

"I thought you liked me behind you, my lady."

Heat shot through her and she swallowed, forcing herself not to climb the male here in front of all three dragon-riding units. She met his smoldering gaze and she could almost taste the salt of his skin on her tongue.

"I'll be at the tavern early," he said. "If you'd like to talk before the others arrive, I'd enjoy that."

Her face hurt from the massive smile spreading over her lips. "Of course. I'll clean up and be right over."

CHAPTER 2
TAHLIA

Tahlia hurried to the assigned bedchamber she shared with her squire, Fara. When she swung open the heavy oaken door, Fara was gripping a tunic and swearing at it. A bowl of water sat on the table under the high window. Soap suds glistened in the light of the wall sconce.

"I don't think you can actually strangle fabric, my friend." Tahlia flopped onto her small bed and toed her boots off.

"It will not release this wine stain and I'm a failure as a squire. You need to go shopping. You can't go around the castle grounds during your off hours looking like a drunken sot."

"I don't care what anything thinks. I'm a knight now. They won't kick me out for a stain."

Her purple face screwed up into a scowl of frustration, Fara threw down the tunic and helped Tahlia unlace the sides of her stiff leather vest. "I didn't plan to be your squire, but I like this position. I don't want anyone to think I'm terrible at it. Your mess reflects on me."

Tahlia chuckled. "Oh, right. Sorry. I'll try not to spill tonight."

"I do have another interest though."

"Other than the dragons and working as a squire?"

Fara nodded. "In addition to being your permanent squire."

"Let me guess. Baking."

Snorting, Fara shook her head. "I could be talked into that. Especially testing our bakes, but that isn't what's on my mind. I have been talking to Healer Albus. He gave me a book about all the medicinal herbs, flowering shrubs, and trees in our kingdom. I've been reading it when you're being insane in the sky."

"But you're not serious about becoming a Healer, are you?"

Fara shrugged.

Fara tended to shift from interest to disinterest in a subject very easily. This was likely just another fleeting moment of curiosity.

"Where are you headed?" Fara asked. "I thought it was an eat-in-your-room night."

Most nights, they dined in the great hall with everyone in the keep. Some days, the staff took time for their families, and the knights and squires made do in their chambers with a tray left by the castle cooks.

"The Brass Lantern. The knights are going to celebrate our day of training. I won the last feat, by the way."

Fara nodded, smiling. "Of course you did. Did it tick off Ophelia?"

"She wasn't in practice again today." Marius had ordered her to take some time to reevaluate her relationship with her dragon because she'd been using these awful spiked gloves on the poor beast.

"Ah, too bad. I would have liked to have a good story about her rage."

"Her rage is pretty legendary from what I've heard."

"Has Marius found out anything else about your poisoner?"

Tahlia chewed her lip, thinking of that day during the tournament. A shudder rippled through her. "He agrees that Ophelia would make a good suspect, but there is no proof. We can't accuse her unless we find some. I'm trying to let it go. I need to focus on training and getting the other knights to feel good about me being here."

"You're just going to let murder go?" Fara raised an eyebrow.

"Sure," Tahlia said, pulling her tunic off. "I'm not dead. Whoever it was failed and now I'm a knight, not just a competitor. They won't try it again." She went to the second bowl of water on their shared table and splashed her face.

"I wish I was as delusionally optimistic as you."

Tahlia dried her face and moved on to her underarms. "Is delusionally a word?"

Fara took Tahlia's second pair of boots from the corner and set them down in front of her. "It is now."

"All right, then. Will you help me with this?" She pointed to her tangled mess of hair.

Fara drew an invisible circle, indicating that Tahlia

should turn around. Tahlia did so and Fara went to work on a new braid.

"You need to grow it out so we can have more fun with styles," Fara said, her fingers moving quickly over Tahlia's head.

"I might have black hair like you, but when mine grows past this point, it's a nightmare. Not all of us have silky locks, my friend." Tahlia's hair brushed her shoulders at this length, but it was long enough to tie back.

Fara made a humming sound and sectioned the front of Tahlia's tresses. "I could help you with that."

"Thanks," Tahlia said, "but I like it short."

"Fine. But you could catch an ague up in the cold air without a heavy braid wrapping that head of yours."

Tahlia tried to turn and give Fara a look, but her friend tugged gently on her hair to keep her head straight.

"I don't think that's a real threat, Fara."

Fara's hands paused in their work. "I know dozens of people who have died of an ague!"

"Dozens?"

"Well, all right, just one. My cousin's great aunt."

"You're comparing my ability to fight off sickness with a random great aunt's."

A "humph" came from Fara. "If you are fine with dying, then so be it."

Tahlia rolled her eyes. "If I promise to grow it for the winter, will you stop pestering me?"

"Maybe."

"Probably not, though?" Tahlia asked, elbowing Fara a little in the thigh.

"You need my warnings." Fara bumped Tahlia's arm with her knee. "You don't take anything seriously enough."

"At least you've moved on from warning me away from dragon riding."

"I recognize a lost cause when I see one." Fara's voice softened. "It's truly amazing, what you've accomplished." She finished the braid with a few pins.

Tahlia faced her, touching the tight coils. "Thank you. For everything." She hugged her, not just for the praise and the braiding, but for the way she'd stood by her every step of the way up this mountain. Literally and figuratively.

The Brass Lantern wasn't too loud yet. The night was young and most ate later on. Tahlia walked in and the warmth of the fire across the room cocooned her immediately. Severin, one of the gate guards, played dice with two others at a round table near the front windows. Good thing Fara had stayed back. She'd be over there losing their new income as quickly as it came in.

Two servers moved around the tavern with trays of mead and bowls of stew. Five males and one female huddled at the bar top, their laughter loud.

Marius was sitting at the table where he'd interviewed Tahlia before the tournament. She paused just to watch him, standing behind a cluster of maids enjoying some time off.

Marius held that same scarlet writing book—a tidily bound collection of parchment—he'd been jotting notes in that day. His brow furrowed as he wrote something down, then crossed it out. He switched his quill to his other hand and stretched his wrist. He had his hair down, and a sheet of it draped over his shoulder as he scribbled more lines of black ink. Her fingers longed to touch his smooth skin, to feel the heat at the crook in his elbow and the underside of his strong jaw.

CHAPTER 3
MARIUS

Marius finished his mead, the honey flavor pleasant—unlike his mood. Tahlia would arrive at any moment and he had yet to finalize the questions he wished to ask her. Of course, he wouldn't sit here and read them aloud, but he needed to see them listed out before launching into conversation. If he didn't have a plan, they'd wander into talking about riding and missions. He longed to know her more deeply than that. Lists tended to calm him, but this time, he was far, far away from a peaceful state of mind. His palms were sweating and he couldn't stop fidgeting.

1. If you could change one thing in your past, what would you alter?
2. Do you long to travel when you're on leave? If so, where and why?
3. ...

Three was the problem. He'd written and rewritten it a dozen times and couldn't get the wording right. He'd wanted to ask her about having younglings, but it was a question that could give him away. If he asked that directly, she would see how serious he was about her. He wasn't certain she felt even close to the same way. Perhaps she'd only enjoyed their night together for the physical pleasure of it. Perhaps her heart wasn't affected as his was. Perhaps she would reject his attempts to make her his mate.

"Oh, and what is the subject for tonight's scarlet book of secrets?"

Tahlia's voice sent a thrill through him, and he braced himself to look up and meet her gorgeous dark honey eyes. When he did, she smiled and set a hand on her hip. The feral side of him wanted to pick her up and throw her onto the table right here, right now. Why did she drive him so mad?

"What has the Shadow of the Shrouded Mountains running his hand through his hair and nibbling his quill like a raccoon?" she asked.

Tahlia leaned to peer at his list. He snatched up the little book and slipped it into the soft leather pocket of the simple vest he wore over his tunic. A part of him wished he could wear battle leathers all the time. He always felt too exposed in civilian clothing.

He gritted his teeth. "It's nothing." Damn. He'd practically growled at her. Taking a deep breath, he gestured to the seat across from him. "Please. Thank you for coming before the others."

"I'm glad you asked me to," she said. "Now, what did you want to chat about?"

Marius motioned to the passing server. "What would you like to drink?"

"Is the mead good?" she asked Marius.

He tapped his empty cup. "Very."

"I'll take one, please," she said to the server.

The male nodded, his gaze sliding from her full lips to her breasts. "Anything else?"

"Just the drink," Marius snapped viciously, a snarl following his words.

Tahlia and the server both stared at Marius, then the server inhaled, blinked, and scurried away like the rat he was.

"You didn't have to scare the poor thing to death just for eyeing me up."

"It's not appropriate," Marius said.

Tilting her head, she lifted her pert nose. She seemed to be peering down at him even though he was a few heads taller. "Because I'm a knight or because of some other reason?"

He fought a growl that tried to crawl up his throat. "I, well, both."

"Both what?"

"Damn it, Tahlia."

"Whoa." She spread her hands. "What is happening?"

He shook himself. "I'm sorry. I'm just…"

"You're nervous, aren't you?" she asked.

"Stop looking like that pleases you so much."

She acted at wiping the smile from her rosy mouth. "Sorry. I'll try."

He swallowed and looked at the grain of the table. "Let's start over."

"All right. Are you Marius now or High Captain?"

"Marius."

She touched his hand briefly, then tucked her hands into her lap. Her smile was back and the beauty of it made his heart ache.

"You weren't nervous about flirting with me in the arena," she said.

Her cheeks flushed, but she didn't seem concerned. His mind, however, was a storm. His thoughts whirled, the questions he'd planned and his plans to murder the server with the roving gaze tangled into a grand mess.

"What do you want?" he spat out, immediately irritated with himself for acting like a troll.

"Umm. You'll have to give me some details about what you mean."

Gods, she was laughing at him. Silently, but still. Her eyes said it all. "If you could change one thing about your past, what would you alter?"

Her bottom lip stuck out a fraction, and her eyes focused on the space above his head. "Oh, good question." Her face cleared and she met his eyes. "Nothing."

"Nothing?"

"Every rough experience I've been through has worked to make me the dragon rider I am today. I don't regret the challenges. I would be a marshmallow without them. I know I would. I adore the pleasant things in life a little too much."

Had he heard her correctly? "What is a marshmallow?"

"A square of fluff made from sap and honey and, well, it's a piece of the dessert afterlife if there is such a place. But you must burn the marshmallow to a crisp. Only way to eat them," she said.

"I feel like I've had ten meads rather than one. What are you talking about?"

Tahlia waved off his confusion like one does a cloud of gnats. "What I meant is that I am fine with my past as is. How about you?"

She must have had an easy life before coming to the mountain.

"I can tell from your expression that you think I'm naive. Let me assure you that I'm not. My family life growing up was not pretty. At all."

Pain tightened the edges of her eyes and her hands had balled on the table. He wanted to cover her fingers with his and comfort her, but was that too much?

Needing something to do with his hands, he tapped his cup in a steady rhythm. "I do believe you're right about difficulties in life, but I couldn't give up the chance to have my sister back."

Her open look said she was listening, patiently waiting for him to speak. His chest tightened and he cleared his throat.

"Pirates ravaged our home and killed her," he said. "Bellona was her name. She is the reason I am here. She gave up her place at a healing arts academy to fund my training with the money we inherited when my parents died."

"I'm so sorry you lost her. It's all the more impressive that you managed to rise to the rank of captain after suffering that loss."

"Thank you." It hadn't been difficult telling her about Bellona. Was the only difference that he was confiding in her instead of trying to pluck information from her? He had to laugh silently at himself. He had been treating her like someone he had to question for order business.

"What else do you want to learn about me?" she asked.

"I'll stop questioning you. I didn't intend for this to be some sort of strange interrogation. I'm just, well, I'm not the best at intimate relationships."

She grinned. "No surprise there, big fella."

"What do you mean?"

"You're not the cozy up-and-chat type."

He wished he was.

"But I like you just how you are, Marius. So ask me whatever you had planned."

His heart did a quick triple beat. "You knew I was mapping out our conversation?"

"I guessed." She jerked her chin and eyed the vest pocket that held his notebook.

It was a relief that she was fine with the way he operated. "All right, then, little salty, where would you travel if you had free time to do so? Or are you more of the type who wants to read by the hearth at home?"

Her eyebrows lifted. "Salty?"

"There is a plant that thrives in the harsh, salt-dense soil of the flats outside my hometown. Its true name is the *schrenkiella parvula*, but we always call it *salty*. You enjoy flourishing in difficult scenarios, so the nickname fits in my mind."

Tahlia laughed, and it was the loveliest sound in all the realms. "Fine. I'm salty, but if you're going to nickname me, I get to do the same to you."

"I already have too many ridiculous monikers," he said.

"None from the one you are considering to be your mate."

He stared.

"Don't look so shocked. Why else would you be giving me a rundown like this? It's so you. You like order. Control. You make weighed decisions. Never reckless. It only makes sense that you would want to find out more about me if you plan a repeat of our night together."

"But it was only one night of passion." How would she react to such a pointed statement?

"Oh, no, it wasn't. I felt a connection with you and you felt it too."

"How can you be so sure? We risk disturbing the order by considering one another as a potential mate."

"You considered Ophelia. Is this only more of a problem because I'm half-human and new?"

"Yes. That's exactly why."

"Maybe tonight will help smooth things over? Do you think my whole unit will come?"

He nodded. "I do."

"Because you asked them to," she said, cocking her head to the side.

"Yes."

"The order is lucky to have you," she said. "Do you think you'll be the next commander?"

"It would be arrogant for me to say yes."

"But silly for you to say no, right? You have to be Gaius's choice."

"Commander Gaius," he corrected. Gods, she had to start using the proper titles.

"I thought we were just Marius and Tahlia at the moment."

He was torn between wanting to be casual and easy with her and teaching her the proper way for a Mist Knight to behave. "Still."

She held out her hands. "Fine. Sorry. Commander Gaius's choice."

"He hasn't said anything yet."

"Do you want the position?" she asked.

He took a slow breath. "Yes, but I will be in the sky, unlike him. I would have to run the order in my way, not his. He knows that."

She ran a fingertip from his elbow to his knuckles. His skin pebbled in the wake of her touch and heat poured through his veins.

"Are you certain we need to spend the evening with the other knights?" she asked. "Because I have some pretty solid ideas on what we could do instead."

He chuckled, surprising himself. She made him feel lighter than anyone else. "Can you wait an hour?"

"I suppose." Her smile was the brightest fire in the room.

CHAPTER 4
TAHLIA

Marius opened his mouth to say something, but the tavern door swung wide and the three captains walked in. Titus's bulky form momentarily blocked Maiwenn and Ewan from view. Titus seemed to be finishing a story.

"The dragon took two fingers before the pirate relented and gave up the sack of grain. I told him he was lucky he'd chosen those particular appendages."

Maiwenn snorted. "True." She had a willowy build and moon-white hair like Marius. When she crossed the room, almost every male gazed her way.

Ewan smoothed a hand over his bald head as he grinned. The oil lamps suspended from the rough-hewn ceiling beams flashed in his eyes. Their unique purple-blue color was even more striking against his dark skin.

Claudia and Justus appeared out of the growing tavern crowd too. Claudia had skin the color of the sunset and a long tail. When Tahlia was a youngling, she had been envious of the Fae who ended up with tails.

Claudia's whipped around behind her, making her look like a wild forest creature. All right. Tahlia was still envious. Tails were just fantastic.

Justus was a mess as usual. His tunic had a tear at the shoulder and he'd somehow splattered mud all up his tall boots even though they hadn't had rain in days.

Titus, Claudia, and Justus made up the rest of unit one, along with Tahlia and Marius. Though Marius, of course, didn't function as a regular member of the unit since he was High Captain. He just usually flew with unit one.

The barkeep hurried over, his face sweating, but his smile genuine. "Greetings, knights! We will arrange the seating as you see fit and I'll have my best server right over to take your orders."

Marius thanked the man and the group settled on chairs, stools, and benches near two tables drawn together. Soon, they had meads all around, a plate of olives and cheese, and three large loaves of fresh bread.

Tahlia was grateful that her whole unit had come, even if it had been because of Marius's request. She wished all the knights were here, but at least they had the unit two and three captains. She had to get Maiwenn on her side.

"I haven't forgotten about the cliff climb training tomorrow at noon," Tahlia said, leaning past Titus to speak to Maiwenn.

Maiwenn's eyes were ice. "Good."

"How is the training going?" Marius asked Maiwenn.

Turning away from Tahlia, Maiwenn set her jaw. She

took a breath. "Very good, despite my misgivings, High Captain."

"And what misgivings are those?"

Maiwenn picked at a flaw in her mug's handle. "I'd rather not say at the moment."

"We can't clear away problems by ignoring them, Lady Maiwenn."

Tahlia wiped her sweaty palms on her trousers. "Just tell me. I'm not afraid of constructive criticism."

"I thought you'd be worthless in the feats of strength and endurance, human."

Everyone froze, Titus with his mug halfway to his mouth and Marius's hand hovering over the olives.

Maiwenn's nostrils flared. "I only speak the truth. She is human. Though she has done well flying and in many of our training scenarios, there is no way she will be as useful as a full Fae when it comes time to fly north."

"You believe Queen Revna and King Lysanael made a mistake in pushing for her survival?"

"No, of course not. But that doesn't prove she belongs in the order. Humans are weak. Selfish. They are not dragon riders."

The silence at the tables rang in Tahlia's ears. Gods, she hadn't thought the female's attitude toward her was that terrible. How wrong she had been...

"I agree with Lady Maiwenn," Claudia said, looking into her mead. "She can lie."

Tahlia struggled to take a breath. "That doesn't mean I will. I can prove to you all that I am worthy."

Marius flattened his palm on the table, then curled

his fingers into a tight fist. "You don't have to. You already have. Once you are a knight, you are a knight."

"Unless you defy orders," Maiwenn said.

Claudia nodded. "Or betray another knight."

Maiwenn stared her down. "Both things that Lady Tahlia, with her human blood, could do without batting an eye."

Tahlia stood, pushing away from the table and looking at each of them in turn. "All I have wanted my entire life is to be here, riding dragons. Ask Fara. She has more Mistgold blood than most of you and can't lie. She can tell you. Why would I ever risk losing my place? Can you believe I would endanger the bond with my dragon?"

"You aren't completely bonded yet," Justus said. At least he had the heart to look sorry for bringing it up.

Enora and Atticus arrived during the tense silence.

Enora's freckles stood out on her fair skin. She glanced from Marius to Maiwenn, who was her unit captain. Atticus bent his head in greeting, his silver horns reflecting the light of the oil lamps.

"What did we miss?" he said, crossing his silver arms.

Breathing out slowly and giving Enora and Atticus a nod to say hello, Tahlia reclaimed her seat. "Listen, if you still feel this way at the end of the season. Any of you. If you want me to leave then, I will."

Enora grimaced, her pale red eyebrows bunching. She squeezed in near Ewan on the bench, and Atticus leaned on the half wall beside her.

"No, you won't," Marius said. "You are a knight now.

You cannot simply leave. We must work out our differences and grow trust as we fly together."

"Knights have been dismissed though, right, High Captain?" Justus said.

Titus leaned back in his chair, his sharp-edged jaw working like he was gritting his teeth. "It would be dishonorable."

"For her." Maiwenn drank the last of her mead.

"For us," Titus corrected. "Dismissal is a dark spot on the order's history. We choose. We train. We hold fast."

Maiwenn stood up and glanced at Claudia. "We are admitting humans now. Our order is changed. We have altered the rules. The moment our king lowered himself to marry one of them," she said, giving Tahlia a flat look, "the whole realm has gone to shite."

She strode away, Claudia joining her.

Sweat trickled down Tahlia's back. She'd thought the other riders, except Maiwenn, were coming around, but obviously Claudia and Justus were less than thrilled at her presence. She was pretty sure Titus was on her side and maybe Ewan. But what about Atticus and Enora? What about the riders who hadn't even shown up tonight? Marius had led her to believe it had only been a secret order to unit one, so the others weren't in defiance of the High Captain or anything, but they weren't here and their absence spoke volumes.

Titus whistled through his teeth quietly. "Well, that was dramatic."

"Treason usually is," Ewan said. "Will you report her, High Captain?"

Enora hummed. "That wasn't really treason."

"It was close enough," Atticus said. Then he exchanged a whisper with Enora and they both glanced at Tahlia.

Marius's eyes flashed with restrained rage. "I'm not reporting anyone."

Tahlia felt a tiny bit bad about how much she loved how angry he was on her behalf.

"We need time to heal this order," he added. He took a pull from his mug, then set it back down and eyed her over the rim. "We will be stronger for it when we are through this challenge."

Ewan nodded as Enora, Justus, and Atticus murmured words of agreement.

Tahlia had to improve the mood. She hated conflict like this. "If that's done for this evening, can we play some dice?"

Ewan clapped his hands once and laughed loudly. "Aye. Now, this is what I came here for."

A ghost of a smile crossed Justus's mouth, but his eyes were cold.

Marius gave Tahlia a measured look. He had more to say on the topic if she had to guess, but he seemed all right with letting it go for now.

Taking the dice from one of the small bags tied to her belt, Tahlia looked over her shoulder to make certain Fara, who had a serious weakness for gambling, hadn't slipped in. "Let's start the pot at two gladecoins."

"Can we play the night version of Fly or Die?" Atticus asked, grabbing another stool to sit on.

"Sure. Threes are wild?" Tahlia wasn't certain how

they played the basic dice game up here on the mountain.

Atticus went over the rules, politely addressing everyone, even though all knew it was only for Tahlia. She felt more of an outsider than ever. She knew so little about the culture here. Maybe she needed to talk to Fara about it. She knew more.

The game went on, everyone taking a turn, losing and betting as they went. The tray of food was polished off. The barkeep brought out bowls of stew and a bottle of crystal wine.

"Ewan, you must have some sort of blessing from the Old Ones." He'd been rolling pretty much perfect numbers. She leaned toward Marius. "You should bet big against him on this round. He's due for a fall, surely."

Marius glanced at her, amusement brightening his eyes. "I don't do *reckless*."

That voice. The low sound of it in that whispering tone turned her stomach into a thunder of tiny dragons flitting from side to side.

"Not even in a game?" she asked.

"Never."

She drummed her fingers on the table. "What if recklessness was the only way to win?"

"I do sometimes act in a way that is not likely to succeed," Marius said. "It's oftentimes required in battle. But I always consider every angle first, therefore avoiding reckless action."

The way she wanted to see him lose control... She licked her lips, blinked, and took another drink of mead.

"Now Ewan," Marius said, "he is more like you, Tahlia."

"I am?" Ewan tossed the dice and watched them land, eyes like a hawk. A one and a five. "Damn." He pushed a gladecoin into the pot at the center of the table.

"You delight in taking risks and perhaps enjoy games a fraction more than the usual knight. Would you agree?" Marius asked Ewan.

Ewan shrugged and grinned at Tahlia. "I guess so."

"Definitely," Titus said.

Marius nodded and slid the dice toward himself. He gathered them and threw his roll. Two sevens and a three.

A cheer went up and Marius collected the coins. "Patient application of probability and reason always win in the end."

"That line isn't as rousingly inspiring as you might think," Tahlia teased.

Marius narrowed his eyes in her direction, but his lips twitched like he wanted to laugh like everyone else was. Well, except Justus, who had gone quiet after Maiwenn and Claudia's departure.

The evening was fun. Marius relaxed and their conversation wove its way through favorite pastimes as younglings to first loves. The riders shared stories of victories and of their first flights.

"Ragewing tried to kill me the first time I rode him."

Tahlia laughed along with the others as she rolled the dice. Ugh. Another set of singles. "Really?"

"He was rather dedicated to my death, yes," Marius said.

"But why would he choose you and then want to be rid of you?"

"Maybe it was a matter of instinct versus desire. His dragon soul called to my soul, as it does in a strong bond. But he desired to remain independent. He was torn."

They played three more rounds, gobbled down a plate of spiced nuts, then everyone broke off and headed to their chambers for sleep.

Marius led Tahlia along the dark streets and through the firelit corridors of the keep.

"I lost some money I didn't know I had tonight," Tahlia said, laughing.

"I might have pushed a silver your way a time or two."

"How naughty of you, High Captain."

He took her hand as they climbed the staircase to his floor. "Would you like to stay the night with me?"

"I thought you'd never ask."

His hand ran up and down her back and her breath lodged between one rib and the next. She swallowed, her body warming.

"Once we get there, you should take charge," he said, his voice silky and achingly alluring in the darkness.

"We will take turns."

They rounded the corner, and he kissed her temple quickly. "Already comfortable ordering me about, I see."

He dismissed his guards and unlocked the chamber door. The scent of Marius along with the perfume of lemons—possibly from cleaning—drew her inside.

"Will you make me a drink?" she asked, giddy with nerves, her body humming with desire.

"Of course, little salty."

CHAPTER 5
TAHLIA

Marius's chambers boasted a grand view of the starry sky. She stood looking out at the silver sparks of light as Marius poured her a crystal goblet of watered wine, then made one for himself. She drank it all in one go, enjoying the slight burn of the liquid down her throat.

"Titus is so good at those mock dives," she said thinking of training. "I need to work on that."

"You'll get there. And you'll get there faster than Titus ever could have dreamed when he was a recruit."

"Thanks, but I don't know." Tahlia ran a finger over the rim of the goblet. "I find it tough to focus on that movement when I have to watch my surroundings."

"You don't quite trust your unit yet. That's understandable."

"I do. Well, except maybe for Maiwenn."

"You don't truly trust the other riders." He drained his goblet and put it on the square table by his ridiculously massive bed. He tapped Tahlia's forehead. "Up here, yes, you trust them, but in here," he said, placing one large finger above her heart, "you aren't there yet. It'll take a battle or a difficult mission for your heart to believe fully in your fellow riders."

"And that's normal?"

Taking her goblet and setting it beside his, he gave her a rare smile. It stole her breath. Sunrises had nothing on a Marius smile.

"Completely typical of a new knight." Taking her hand in his, he kissed each one of her fingertips. Then he pulled her close and held her. She melted into the divine warmth of his arms and the feel of his strength.

"You fly like a goddess," he whispered, his breath hot on the shell of her ear.

Satisfaction curled like a cat around her heart. "You're not so bad yourself."

A quiet hum of amusement echoed in his broad chest.

"Now," she said, stepping back a little and looking him over. "I seem to recall someone telling me I could take charge."

He bowed his head and held out a hand, so courtly and full of restrained power. Want crashed over Tahlia and she took an uneven breath. He lifted his head and gave her a heated look.

"What do you wish of me, my lady?"

"Remove my clothing, one piece at a time. But we will take turns."

With a wicked grin, he began unlacing her stiff leather vest. When it was loosened sufficiently, he tugged it over her head. He reached for her tunic, but she held up a finger to stop him.

"Ah, ah, ah. We are taking turns, remember?" She started working on the laces of his vest while he ran his hands through her hair, undoing her braids and sending the tie and pins fluttering and clicking to the floor. Every sweep of his palm against her scalp sent wonderful shivers down her neck. Together, they maneuvered his vest free.

Next, he unbuckled her belt and threw it down. He slipped her tunic off, his eyes glittering with want. She hadn't worn any upper undergarments today exactly for this surprise moment. She knew her breasts weren't the most luscious in the kingdom by any stretch, but they seemed to do the job, and she was proud to bring out that feral look in such a disciplined male.

"Tahlia..." Marius's voice had dropped to a gravelly tone that usually meant he was losing patience.

"Now yours." She pointed to his tunic.

Growling, he ripped his in two and threw it beside her hairpins. "My lady." His words sounded like an order and a plea twisted into one.

"And the belt. Oh, and go ahead and remove those boots and trousers. Maybe put the boots back on after? Hmm." She tapped her chin, delighting in the way he violently discarded his belt, tugged off his trousers and boots, shed his short pants, then slid his boots back on. He was following her orders, but tension rolled from him in waves that made Tahlia's thighs clench in anticipation.

Another growl issued from the High Captain as he

stood before her in nothing but his boots. "You have tested me enough, my lady."

His body was worthy of all the gossip surrounding him. Black and gold inkings trailed down the hard-wrought muscles of his chest and abdomen. It was wild how narrow his waist was considering how incredibly large he was. She ran her hands down the smooth, warm skin of his torso, and he pulled in a quick breath, his head falling back.

"My lady," he begged. "Please."

Cheeks and chest flushing, she set her fingers along his sharp hipbones. Heat flooded her body, her bones going liquid. She eyed one of his more...fascinating areas. "Are all males with Mistgold blood this, umm, blessed?"

He snarled and lunged, lifting her and landing on the bed in one breathtaking movement. His weight sank into her. It was the greatest sensation. He pinned her to the cloud-like duvet with his hips; the pressure from his obvious desire for her threw sparks of pleasure over her flushed skin. A moan escaped her. Gods, he felt amazing.

His lips claimed hers as he bent his head to kiss her chest. His tongue flicked over the peak of her breast and around and under, here and there, making her squirm beneath him. She gripped his moon-white hair in rough handfuls. Arching against him, savoring the friction of his body on hers, she whispered his name.

With surprisingly careful movements, he moved on to taking off her boots and leather trousers.

He stopped, inhaling sharply. She hadn't worn any undergarments below the navel either. His mouth came down on her hip, his tongue touching the hot skin there and lower. Pleasure simmered in her blood and her heart pounded so loudly she knew he could hear it. But she wasn't overly worried about it. He cared deeply for her, and while they weren't mated yet, she dared to hope. A little overexcitement on her part surely wouldn't ruin the whole thing.

Kissing a trail between her thighs, his hands wandered around the back of her knees. He shifted her up, closer, and her breath caught. His hair fell over her hips and stomach, tickling her as his mouth drew pleasure from her body like a bard draws music from a lute. She could die now and be happy forever, honestly. His hands slid down and he gracefully took off her boots and socks. His thumb circled the center of her heel and moved upward, eliciting a gasp from her.

"I order you to take command now," she whispered, feeling powerful and incredibly grateful for finding him —her friend, her shelter, her challenge.

A smile like a sword's edge glimmered along his lips, showing his fangs. He bent and lifted something from the floor. He held it up and raised his eyebrows. His whip.

CHAPTER 6
TAHLIA

The milky light of pre-dawn streamed from the high window and poured over Marius's well-muscled chest. Tahlia skimmed her fingertips across his body, her head full of delicious dreams. She lifted her cheek from Marius's shoulder, and he smiled down at her, looking like a completely different version of his normally stern self. His hand cradled her face, his skin warm and perfect. She had definitely perished and moved on to a glorious afterlife.

A knocking sounded through Marius's chambers, and Tahlia growled, sitting up.

"You sound like me," Marius said, laughter in his storm-gray eyes. He slipped out of bed and drew on a pair of linen trousers he had folded by his armoire. "I'll take care of it. You rest."

Tahlia rubbed her face as Marius left the bedroom. "Punch that person for me, please."

A chuckle echoed from the outer chamber, then the door creaked open. Low voices spoke in quick sentences.

Tahlia scrambled out of bed, pulling a small woolen blanket around her and peering out the half-open bedchamber door. The male at the door wore the commander's sigil of the crescent moon and sword.

"Commander Gaius requests your presence immediately. Both of you, High Captain, Lady Tahlia."

Marius faced Tahlia and gave her a meaningful look, pursing his full lips slightly.

She waved a hand. "It's all right. Let's go. I don't want to cause any more problems that might result in you standing in front of a dragon and waiting for the flame." She still could hardly comprehend he had risked that for her.

The messenger nodded to Marius and left.

Marius shut the door and eyed Tahlia. "Yes, you do."

"Do what?" she asked.

Marius passed her, dropping a kiss on her forehead. "Cause more problems. It's your favored pastime, I believe."

Tahlia giggled. "It really is."

Shaking his head, Marius dressed in his leathers and Tahlia did her best to keep her hands off him. Once she was dressed as well, they walked hurriedly down the corridor, past a few other knights and staff.

"So he asked for me too?" Tahlia smoothed her hair back—a lost cause. It was tangled into a knot at the back of her skull. "Do you know what this might be about?"

"No. It could simply be mission information and he heard we were together last night."

"Together." Tahlia grinned and rubbed the spot

where Marius's whip had been wound around her wrist. "In so many ways."

He gave her a very Marius look, cold and formidable. She shivered, delighted.

"Lady Tahlia, I must insist you hold your tongue."

"On your—"

Fara and Remus, Marius's squire, rounded the corner and nearly mowed them down.

"Apologies, sir, lady!" Remus bowed low.

Fara's purple face flushed. She grimaced and curtseyed repeatedly. She thought Mist Knights walked around constantly on the verge of murder. Courage wasn't her strength. But loyalty was and Tahlia couldn't have become a dragon rider without her.

"All is well." Marius lifted a hand, dismissing their apologies.

"We were at the stables working and heard you were called to see the commander, so we wanted to check if you needed us to do anything or to accompany you," Remus said.

Marius glanced at Tahlia, who shrugged. "Walk with us," he said, facing Remus and Fara again. "We'll see if the commander requires specific actions."

The males dropped back to discuss the plan Titus had suggested yesterday concerning the upcoming pirate raids in the north.

Fara popped her knuckles and looked at Tahlia, the whites of her eyes showing all around her slitted irises. "How was the tavern? Please only tell me the good parts. And slow down and let me do something with this hair of yours."

"The tavern was good. Except for a few grouches."

Braiding and pinning Tahlia's locks. Fara bent close to her ear. "Are you still certain you want to be a Mist Knight? Because I truly believe we could open up a vicious Leatherworker shop in town."

"Exactly how could making purses and satchels be vicious?"

Fara patted Tahlia's finished braid, then came up beside Tahlia. "We would slay the competition."

Tahlia snorted. "Not literally?"

"No, you blood-thirsty miscreant. With our high-quality skills."

Tahlia tilted her head and clicked her tongue. "Skills neither of us have."

"We will have them."

"I'm not giving up dragons for arts and crafts, Fara."

"Come on. It's cozy in town. Less wind. Fewer things that want to eat you."

"Bluewing doesn't want to eat us," Tahlia said, thinking of yet another possible name for her Seabreak dragon.

Fara wrinkled her nose. "I don't think that's the name. Did you ask her about Stormwave?" She meant had Tahlia asked the dragon. The Seabreak did have a way to communicate with Tahlia. Because they were almost fully bonded, just a head nod or a snort could tell Tahlia what the Seabreak was thinking.

"She didn't go for it."

Fara narrowed her eyes. "Maybe your dragon should try to be less picky."

Tahlia leaned closer to Fara and whispered, "I'm not sure what this little meeting will entail."

"Maybe he uncovered information about who poisoned you?" Fara glanced at Tahlia as they kept on down the corridor where the sunrise was just beginning to cast pink and orange over the windowsills, the walls, and the floor. Fara's pupils were fully slitted because her blood was almost completely Fae, like Marius. Tahlia's were not quite the same shape because she was half-human. During the competition to become a Mist Knight, that human blood had resulted in someone poisoning her and had landed her in front of the execution dragon to be roasted. Thankfully, she had come through after a twist-turn of events.

"I would love it if the commander had some information." An uneasy feeling crawled through Tahlia's stomach. She wanted to find out, but if it hadn't been a competitor who was now long gone, off the mountain, then the poisoner was still here.

The corridor opened into the keep's foyer. The home to the Order of the Mist Knights was more mountain than hand-built structure. Towers rose from rough stone and massive crystals—some as clear as a summer day and others of rosy pink, sage green, ocean blue, gold, and indigo—crowned the castle at various entrances and balconies.

The stained glass and crystals scattered light across the foyer's tapestries and wide stone steps. The rose-hued crystals had given Marius and Tahlia some delightful trouble toward the end of the competition. An earthquake in the valley had activated them. Since

Marius and Tahlia had a natural attraction to one another, the crystals' mating magic, which was usually reserved for dragons, had poured over Tahlia and Marius, bringing them together more quickly than was normal.

Tahlia didn't regret it one bit.

Beyond the keep's foyer, the great hall bustled with activity. The water clock chimed the hour as they crossed the tiled floor and headed for the first of three corridors. Two guards opened double doors leading to the platform that worked on a pulley system to reach the commander's chambers.

The guards nodded in respect to Marius and Tahlia. The taller of the two glanced at Remus and Fara. "Only the High Captain and Lady Tahlia have been invited."

"I'll see you at the stables?" Fara asked Tahlia.

"Sounds good," Tahlia said.

Fara gave them each a curtsey, then left.

Remus gave Marius and Tahlia a bow and followed Fara.

As soon as the squires were gone, Tahlia asked the question burning her tongue. "Do you think the commander has information about the poisoner?"

Light from the passing floors blinked across the small space.

"That is my dearest wish, I assure you," he said. "It would make sense considering he has invited you."

"But it could be about..." Tahlia wiggled her eyebrows.

"Perhaps," he said, looking straight ahead as the platform trembled slightly and lifted them higher and higher.

He had his serious face on again, back to being the High Captain.

She slid a hand over his thigh and watched the next floor pass by. He tensed, and in her periphery, he shot her a reprimanding look. It was only encouraging really. She dragged her palm higher on his leg. His large fingers closed over hers, sending sparks up her arm, then he moved her hand to her thigh. She fought a smile. Breaking through his orderly way of life was her second-favorite activity. Of course, dragon riding was number one.

A memory of the first time they'd met flashed through Tahlia's mind. Marius had been standing with Ragewing in the arena, his Fae-white hair lifting slightly in the breeze, the muscles along his exposed arms rolling under his sun-touched skin. His gaze had been that of a hawk's, focused and deadly serious. Immediately, the urge to ruffle his feathers, to break that concentration, had surged inside her. She'd wanted to see him undone a little and that was even before she knew that he was the great Shadow of the Shrouded Mountains, a figure that meant death for anyone who dared to cross the border without good cause and the male who had ripped apart scores of pirate crews and their ships with his exacting strategy and fierce courage. Once she'd realized he was the High Captain, that urge had only grown stronger.

The memory of the first time they'd shared a bed shot heat from her heart to her core. Closing her eyes briefly, she pulled in a shaky breath. Images of his hawk-like gaze near her inner thigh flickered behind her eyes. *I promised punishment for your impertinence,* he had whispered teasingly over her skin as a spark of mischief lit his stormy eyes.

A shiver of desire had crashed over her like a wave. *And what did you have in mind, High Captain?* she had said back. The warmth of his hand sliding up her stomach to cup her breast had been divine, and the way he'd cradled the back of her head and spoken ever so softly into her ear...

The platform came to a stop. Two more guards stood at the door. They bowed their heads as Marius and Tahlia exited, leaving the platform and its echoing shaft. Tahlia glanced at Marius, who gave her a quick wink. She couldn't fight the wide smile that tugged at her lips.

The guards, dressed in Gaius's crescent moon and sword livery, opened the commander's door and stood back for Marius and Tahlia to enter. Tahlia removed her gladius and sheath from her belt and stowed them by the front entrance near a decorative amphora mounted into a wooden frame. Sitting for any length of time with a sword attached to one's waist was awkward. Marius kept his on. Of course, he was used to wearing it since he'd been in the order for years.

Commander Gaius sat in a low-backed, velvet-upholstered chair by the thick glass of his large window. The window looked out on the grounds—the courtyard beyond the foyer, the wall where Marius had first kissed Tahlia under the crystals' influence, and the manicured lawn that led to the cliff edge that the knights sometimes used for takeoff.

Gaius stood as they approached, and they bowed and curtseyed. The commander's normally flushed face was oddly pale, but his hair was still as full as ever, mostly covering his dramatically pointed ears. He nodded to them.

"I understand today is your free day," he said, "so I won't take up much of your time. To put it bluntly, I have a personal request."

Personal? Tahlia glanced at Marius, but his focus was on the commander.

Gaius paced, the sunlight washing over the black tunic he wore when not on duty. "It's Ophelia."

Tahlia's gut twisted. Ophelia, Gaius's daughter, rode in Tahlia's unit, but she'd been out of action ever since Marius reprimanded Ophelia for using spiked gloves on her Green-flanked Terror. And there was also the whole Tahlia-inadvertently-broke-up-their-engagement thing. Tahlia shifted on her feet, but Marius remained as still as stone.

"My daughter still hasn't properly bonded with her dragon, but that moment is not far off."

Marius's eyes and mouth twitched like he wanted to argue, but he held his tongue.

Gaius halted his pacing and stared Marius down even though he was shorter than him. "She remains unhappy with the way your engagement ended, Marius. I can't say that I blame her."

"I apologize for the way I handled that," Marius said to Gaius, his tone sincere.

Marius then glanced at Tahlia, but she wasn't about to say anything close to sorry.

He must have been able to tell she wasn't going to apologize because he squeezed his eyelids shut. The muscle in his jaw worked the way it did when he was frustrated, but his eyes opened to show the smallest twinkle of amusement.

She hadn't planned to fall for Marius, and Ophelia had done her best to keep Tahlia from the order. Ophelia was probably the one who had poisoned her, though Tahlia had zero proof of that. Plus, Ophelia had been cruel to her dragon. Anyone who treated animals poorly deserved to die in Tahlia's not-so-humble opinion.

"I accept your apology," Gaius said to Marius, "but I request that you two keep yourselves, how should I say this... I request that you hold off on your potential mating bond until Ophelia has had time to work through this difficult time."

Potential mating bond. Tahlia wanted to jump in the air and sing a song. But did Marius feel that way toward the idea of their future?

It was silly that Gaius was asking her and Marius to keep a distance. Ophelia was no delicate flower. Was she truly struggling? Tahlia couldn't imagine the proud full Fae female who rode one of the most terrifying creatures in the world being broken by anything.

"Of course, sir," Marius said.

"As you wish, Commander," Tahlia said.

"I must ask," Marius started, "have you gleaned any information about who poisoned Lady Tahlia from your informants?" His nostrils flared, his quiet rage trying to burst through his disciplined exterior. He didn't seem to be too keen on Gaius's request either.

Gaius pressed a fist against his mouth, then let his hand fall as he gazed at Tahlia. "I thought we had a lead on who meant you harm, Lady Tahlia, but I'm afraid I don't yet know. I will send you any information I gather the moment it arrives."

"Thank you," Tahlia said.

"I appreciate this. Both of you, thank you very much," Gaius said.

They nodded in unison, then left the chamber and entered the now empty platform shaft.

"Oh, wait," Tahlia said, recalling her gladius. "Hold on. I forgot my sword."

"I'll go on." Marius studied her face like he was gauging how she would respond to the order they had been given.

"How long do you think he will ask us to stay apart?"

Marius lifted a hand like he wanted to reach for her, but he let his arm fall. "Not an extensive period, I'm sure."

"All right. Fine. I'll see you later, then, I guess."

"Tahlia, you are the light in my day. We will get through this to whatever waits for us on the other side." He took her hand and rubbed the back of it with his thumb.

A smile tugged at Tahlia's frown and a shiver danced over the place where he touched her. "And you're the storm I like to rouse just to see the lightning, High Captain."

He smiled in full, rang the bell for the guards below to work the pulley, and disappeared.

Tahlia returned to the commander's chamber, hoping to slip in and out without notice. She didn't want any more awkward chats with Gaius about Marius or Ophelia. The guards nodded to her and permitted entry.

Inside the front entrance, she bent to retrieve her gladius. A shadow flickered in her periphery. She glanced up to see Ophelia emerge from another room, blue-green hair tightly woven around her head. Ophelia headed toward the back corridor of the apartment. She didn't seem to have noticed Tahlia, thank the Old Ones. Dark swirls and star-white sparks spun along Ophelia's left hand, and an odd floral scent wafted through the chambers. Tahlia blinked and rubbed her eyes. When she looked again, the swirls and sparks were gone. Had she just hit her head too hard in training yesterday? Surely. There wasn't any magic that appeared like that, was there?

She attached the sheathed gladius to her belt and took her turn on the platform, her mind whirling with thoughts of Ophelia, poison, and the fact that she wouldn't get her hands on Marius anytime soon. Gritting her teeth, she headed toward the dragon stables to find Fara and update her on all the goings-on before they had to start on their laundry.

Maiwenn caught her at the entrance to the stables. "Since we are free today, you're going to train with me."

Damn it. She had hoped Maiwenn had forgotten. "Unfortunately, I have laundry to do. I know, so domestic."

Unblinking, Maiwenn didn't crack a smile. "We aren't doing the cliff climbing. I have something else in mind. Meet me in the arena. Now."

Ugh. And this day had started so nicely…

CHAPTER 7
TAHLIA

Tahlia climbed onto her Seabreak's shoulder, holding the edges of the dragon's scales as she moved toward the saddle.

Maiwenn was already mounted on her male Seabreak, Donan. He flapped his four wings, a larger version of the female's set, and huffed into the air. The show of dominance was wasted on Tahlia's dragon. She pranced past him, head high and wings extended like she didn't see him as any sort of leader.

Already sweating, Tahlia took the reins and wished with everything her dragon would curb her rebellious nature for the afternoon. Maiwenn was already going to be horribly mean. She'd proven that in their other training sessions. Tahlia didn't need anything making Maiwenn even less pleased with Tahlia's existence.

"Follow me," Maiwenn said, her Mistgold blood raising her words' volume so that her voice echoed through the arena.

Tahlia and her dragon took off as ordered. A bank of

clouds soaked Tahlia's face and made the saddle slick beneath her. She should have kept her bottom firmly set, but it was tough when Donan flew so fast and Tahlia's dragon was trying to display that she had no problems keeping up.

"You'll lose me if you fly like a maniac, darling," Tahlia said to the Seabreak.

The Seabreak broke through the bank of cover and the sun glittered across her lovely horns.

"First," Maiwenn said as Donan wheeled around to face them, making Tahlia's mount rear and list to the side, "we will run a triangle with an imaginary third. On my count... Three, two, one!"

Donan was a slash of ocean blue in the pale wash of the sky. Tahlia's dragon roared in frustration that Tahlia felt like an itch just beneath her skin. They were not in formation no matter how Tahlia imagined said third rider and dragon.

"She can't fly that fast, Maiwenn. She's trying!"

Maiwenn had Donan turn sharply and they flew overhead, their shadow throwing Tahlia and her dragon into darkness. "Sorry, I can't hear your weak human voice," Maiwenn called out, using that power that only those with hefty amounts of Mistgold in their blood possessed. "Shout louder maybe?"

Tahlia wanted to flip her off and fly away, but she bit her tongue and tapped her Seabreak's neck, urging the dragon to take up one point of the triangle formation.

Before they flew in the right position, another rider burst from the thick strip of clouds.

Tahlia's heart stuttered, and she drew the reins back

to slow her dragon. Maiwenn had Donan pause too; her face was unreadable.

Ophelia.

The female's blue-green hair whipped in the wind. "Good afternoon, riders."

Her Green-flanked Terror snarled and flapped its ratty-edged wings to hover in place.

"Lady Ophelia," Maiwenn said, nodding respectfully.

Gods, how Tahlia wanted to strangle Ophelia. She'd sleep better at night, that was for sure.

And why was Maiwenn acting like they needed to show extra respect for Ophelia? They were all of the same rank. Was Maiwenn behaving that way simply because Ophelia was Commander Gaius's daughter?

Tahlia jerked her chin in a reluctant greeting. She'd be damned if she bowed her head to the one who had likely poisoned her.

Ophelia's grin sent a shiver through Tahlia. "Let's see that triangle formation you were sadly attempting again, shall we?" Ophelia called out.

"No problem." Tahlia's throat burned from trying to shout as loudly as possible over the wind and across the distance between the three riders and their mounts.

Ophelia cocked her head. "I'm so sorry. You'll have to say that again. Didn't catch it."

Tahlia waved her off.

Ophelia shrugged. Maiwenn's Donan took off like a shot. Ophelia's Green-flanked Terror took up the lead spot in the formation with ease, but Tahlia's Seabreak flew hard and couldn't quite hit the right mark. The dragon's sides heaved as she struggled to speed up.

"It's too fast," Tahlia shouted out. "She's not big enough."

"Or is her rider too clumsy?" Maiwenn called back.

So they could hear Tahlia, at least some of the time. She gritted her teeth. It was one thing to bully Tahlia, but they were treating her dragon poorly too.

"You are perfect. They are just being ridiculous," Tahlia said, doing her best to aim her words toward the dragon's ear. The Seabreak twisted its ear toward her, so hopefully she heard and understood.

"Order a new formation, Tahlia!" Maiwenn commanded.

Would double square be a good one? They would still be missing a rider, but it was one they practiced less, so perhaps that would be a good challenge. Or bow and arrow? Then she could call out a drop, which would be easier on her smaller dragon.

"Bow and arrow!"

Maiwenn and Ophelia remained in triangle formation as if they hadn't heard her. The wind had risen, so maybe they weren't just being pricks this time.

"Bow and arrow, then drop on a five count!" Tahlia shouted, trying again.

Ophelia turned her way and blasted forward, taking up the arrowhead point. "Bow and arrow, drop at five!" she shouted in Maiwenn's direction.

Maiwenn steered Donan and soon they were parallel with Tahlia and her mount.

"One, two, three, four..." Tahlia whispered to herself.

She pressed her palm against the Seabreak's scales and the dragon dove. The blue beauty tucked her wings tight and she zipped toward the arena, outpacing Ophelia and forcing the Terror to adjust his head and wings to decrease the influence of the wind on his speed. Ophelia looked over her shoulder and gave Tahlia a smile full of threats. Tahlia swallowed and focused on the quickly approaching ground.

"And up now," Maiwenn ordered.

Tahlia's and Ophelia's mounts moved in sync, drawing their wings wide and using the airspeed to flip directions. Tahlia's body lifted from the saddle, wind whooshing under her and trying to pull her away. She forced her heels down in the stirrups and tightened the hold her legs had on the dragon's mounded spine. The Seabreak turned her head to eye Tahlia and they lost altitude.

"Go on! I'm fine!" Tahlia smiled in what she hoped was an encouraging spirit even though it probably looked like she was about to vomit, which she was.

They caught up and ran three more formations and simulations. Justus and his Spikeback, Longfire, joined them. Every time Tahlia was ordered to run a mock scenario, she had to use hand signals. They either truly couldn't hear her or they were trying to prove the point that half-humans shouldn't be in the sky with them. She could have sworn all three of them were getting her directions wrong on purpose. At one moment, Justus had Longfire blow third fire—a lower level of flame but still rough and not at all what Tahlia had commanded. The fire nearly scorched her Seabreak. Tahlia's blood boiled.

When Maiwenn at last called for landing, Tahlia and her dragon were winded and gasping. On shaky legs,

Tahlia dismounted. She leaned against the Seabreak and ran a hand down the dragon's quickly moving ribs.

"I am sorry they are acting like fiends. It's my fault, and I hate that you're being dragged into this."

The dragon twisted and snuffed into Tahlia's hair, blowing her wind-tangled braid even more out of its pins and ties. Tahlia reached up and scratched the Seabreak under the chin. A deep trill vibrated through the softer scales there and Tahlia's anger and frustration fled in the wake of knowing this majestic creature cared for her and didn't blame her for anything.

Footsteps sounded behind her, and Tahlia turned to see Maiwenn, Ophelia, and Justus looking at her like she was a piece of dragon dung.

"You see?" Maiwenn put a hand on her hip and shook her head. "The fact that you don't have Mistgold blood and aren't even fully Fae means you are a weak link in our unit. I am not trying to hate on you for fun. It's not your fault you're tainted with inferior blood. You can't choose your birth. But it's a fact. And it will get some of us killed. I'd swear on it."

Ophelia's gaze traveled up and down Tahlia as if she was sizing her up for a physical fight. "Where are you from? Don't lie this time, human."

"Northwoods was a lie?" Justus asked.

"It was," Tahlia admitted. She'd indeed lied when she'd competed for her place. She'd told them she was the Lady of Northwoods, a completely imagined name and title. "I was born south of the capital."

Justus's eyes widened.

Ophelia held out a hand. "So you weren't even born near the Shrouded Mountains."

"That doesn't surprise me," Maiwenn said.

"But some of the other riders weren't born here," Tahlia argued.

"They had parents who were and were only temporarily relocated because of their landholdings."

Nodding, Ophelia continued, "You can't possibly fit in with the order. You know nothing of our culture or our ways. The order must function as one body. I am sometimes a fist while Titus is our eyes and Maiwenn serves as a wing."

Tahlia frowned. Ophelia was very good at being horrible, but not so great at metaphors. "Right. It's true. I'm learning. I mean, it's only been fourteen days or so..."

Her glare said she didn't care about the short timeframe. Of course not. That would have been reasonable.

"What festival do we celebrate silently at the end of the year? What sacrifice is required during said festival?"

Tahlia had no clue. She had been studying the Shrouded Mountain culture, a niche community in the Realm of Lights that did indeed do things differently from everyone else. But she hadn't had enough time to learn everything. "I don't know."

"I appreciate you being truthful," Maiwenn said, her tone painfully reluctant. "Do you have any clue about our great library and the ancient magic and history stored there? Have you studied any of the archives yet? Or are you spending most of your free time—"

She abruptly cut herself off, glancing at Ophelia and

appearing to decide not to mention Marius. At least, that was Tahlia's guess.

"I thought the only magic came from the crystals and the vaguely understood power stirring in the dragons' blood and in yours," Tahlia said.

Justus raised an eyebrow. "We used to work Unseelie magic here."

"You did?"

"It was outlawed and for good reason," Maiwenn said. "But you need to know these things. Our sacred days. The proper way to behave as a representative of our mountain. The dangers hiding in our history."

She was mean-spirited, but Tahlia couldn't fault her logic. Ignoring Ophelia's insanely creepy stare, Tahlia addressed Maiwenn. "You're right. I am trying."

"Try harder."

Tahlia glanced at Ophelia who was now looking at her own hand. A red scar, like something she'd received recently, marred her palm.

"Can I go now?" Tahlia asked, directing the question to whomever was really running this show.

Maiwenn gave Ophelia a frown, then faced Tahlia. "Yes, but don't get comfortable. I might send for you."

Justus glared, his gaze like a burn.

Fantastic. Tahlia would probably be in the bathing rooms when Maiwenn popped up again to torture her. Surely, the riders who weren't thrilled with Tahlia's presence would all get over it soon, right?

. . .

During Tahlia's laundry time an hour later, alarm bells rang through the castle grounds.

CHAPTER 8
TAHLIA

In Tahlia and Fara's bedchamber, Fara threw down the tunic she'd been folding. "What is happening?"

"How would I know?" Tahlia asked, tossing a neat stack of socks onto the bed before rushing to the door. "I've been with you, dear friend. Or did you forget I was here in the excitement of our laundry party?" She squeezed out her damp hair with a square of linen as they hurried into the corridor.

Most knights had a servant in addition to a squire, but Tahlia didn't have the funds. Payday hadn't come up yet, as she'd only been a knight for a handful of days, so they had to do their own chores either before sunrise and training began, well after the dinner hour, or during the rare instance of free time.

Fara ran beside Tahlia, her dark lavender face flushed. "I thought maybe you would know something about the emergency through your dragon."

They pounded down the stairs.

"Sadly, no," Tahlia said.

"Maybe it's only a drill. Just to see if we can exit the keep quickly and safely."

"Sure. The order is usually all about keeping everyone safe and cozy."

Fara let out a groan that was part whine as she grasped Tahlia's arm. "Slow down. I'm not as fast as you."

"You should be," Tahlia said. "If you consider your blood versus mine."

Fara narrowed her eyes and cocked her head. "Your training is already showing. Plus, I think bonding to a dragon makes you faster."

"Huh. I had no idea." That was fantastic.

The trumpets sounded again and Tahlia's happy mood dropped away.

They hurried through the foyer, jostled by others doing the same. In the courtyard, all the other knights, squires, and castle staff had gathered. Heads were close together and the buzz of worried conversation was nearly as loud as the wind that buffeted the greenery growing along the walls.

Marius stood at the opening in the low wall, talking to two Healers—one of whom was Albus, the male who had saved Tahlia from the poison and who had discovered she was half-human. Tahlia tried not to resent the fact that Albus had reported her. It was his job, after all.

Tahlia and Fara went to stand by the rest of unit one.

"What is this all about?" Tahlia asked Titus, whose arms were crossed as he studied Marius.

Titus glanced at Tahlia and Fara and nodded in greeting. "The High Captain hasn't said anything yet. But it can't be good."

Dread slithered up Tahlia's spine.

Marius cleared his throat and clasped his hands behind his back. "I have terrible news to report. I never thought this day would arrive so soon. Our Commander Gaius is dead."

Tahlia gripped Fara's hand as a chill swept down her back.

No. They'd just seen Gaius a few hours ago. He had been upset, maybe a little pale, but he had seemed as healthy as anyone.

"It has to be a mistake," Fara said quietly. "Right?"

The other knights grew eerily silent, a mark of how shocked they were.

Marius showed not an ounce of emotion as he addressed the crowd, but Tahlia knew he was crushed. The commander was a father figure to every knight in the Order of the Mist Knights.

Fara chewed her thumbnail and looked wide-eyed around the hushed crowd. "...has to be a mistake."

"High Captain Marius doesn't make mistakes," Claudia said from the other side of Titus.

Marius touched the ring of black adamant he wore on his smallest finger. His steely stare found Tahlia. Her heart jumped, and she expected him to give her a meaningful look, but he grimaced and turned away as if the sight of her hurt him.

He cleared his throat and addressed the crowd again. "Our Healers say that his death happened mid-morning. They don't know the cause, only that there was no obvious wound despite the blood found at the site. Lady Ophelia reported his door was locked and that he wasn't answering her knocking or shouts from outside. She called out, and..." Marius's hand strayed to that ring again and he covered his mouth and cleared his throat once more. "And the castle guards worked the door open."

A twinge of unease bit at Tahlia's heart. Ophelia hadn't been able to get through the door? But she had been there already when Tahlia and Marius had met with Gaius. Had she left and then been unable to return? The commander's door had been unlocked when Tahlia had been there, the chambers open to those people the guards permitted onto the platform.

Titus stepped away from the others and weaved through the churning group of Fae, no doubt heading for Marius.

Tahlia looked around the crowd on tiptoe. "Where is Ophelia now?" she whispered to Fara. "Do you see her anywhere?"

The wind whipped across the courtyard and the scent of rain filled the air.

Fara began searching too, craning her neck to see past Justus's wide frame. "I don't. But she hasn't been around lately anyway, right? She hasn't yet returned to training?"

"Not regular training," Tahlia said, "but she showed up for my session with Maiwenn."

"Why didn't you tell me?"

"I honestly didn't want to dwell on it."

Fara clicked her tongue and pursed her lips. "Laundry is preferable to those two, yes."

"Exactly."

"But why are you asking if I saw her here?"

"Because earlier, before our terrible and oh-so-special training, I saw her in the commander's chambers."

Fara frowned. "You did?"

Marius had started laying out the plans for the funeral, his voice strained with cloaked grief. "...and we will host a Blessing Procession here for the town as is called for considering his position."

Tahlia tilted her head toward Fara. "I'll tell you more later," she said quietly.

Fara's eyes widened, then she nodded. "Understood."

Tahlia had to talk to Marius. He needed to know she'd seen Ophelia in the commander's chambers. That Ophelia had somehow, in some Fae trickster way, lied about not being able to enter her father's rooms. Granted, that deceit didn't mean she'd killed him... After all, Commander Gaius was Ophelia's father. He had cared for her. She didn't have any reason to murder him. Did she? Could she truly be that unhinged about Marius and the breaking of their engagement? And even if she was, why would she take that out on her father, the male who had respected her enough to ask Tahlia and Marius to hold off on their relationship just for Ophelia's sake?

Tahlia tried to meet Marius's eyes, but he had a crowd around him—Healers, Bloodworkers, Remus, Maiwenn, Ewan, Titus... Everyone wanted to give their condolences and needed his input on what would happen next.

Fara scowled at the crowd mulling around Marius. "He should have announced the new commander. It would have been in the death documents sealed in Commander Gaius's lock box."

Tahlia's mind whirled. She climbed onto a boulder embedded in the courtyard lawn to get a better look at Marius.

Who would lead the Mist Knights now? The most sensible choice would be Marius. Tahlia thought of her lock box and how empty it was. She had one small note that whatever money she left when she died would be split evenly between Fara's and Tahlia's mothers, but that was it. She had no grand declarations to include and seal up with wax as the notary watched on. That part of her becoming a Mist Knight had been comically simple and quick.

"It'll be Marius as the next commander," Tahlia said, more to herself than anyone else.

Ophelia's blue-green hair appeared in the crowd. A chill wrapped around Tahlia's body. Stone-faced, Ophelia approached Marius, Titus, Maiwenn, and Ewan —all the unit captains.

Maiwenn's eyebrows rose at Ophelia's approach, but why? Was it because Ophelia wasn't showing grief? But Ophelia was a Mist Knight, a trained warrior who could most likely hold back emotions until she was granted privacy. Also, she was a cold hag who probably only ever wept for herself.

Ewan crossed his arms, face unreadable. His dark

skin was a stark contrast to Maiwenn's pale complexion. He leaned toward Titus, who had fisted one of his big hands over his mouth, assumably to keep anyone from reading his lips.

Ophelia spoke to the small group of leaders, holding out a slip of parchment.

Marius stiffened and blinked as if surprised by the parchment's contents. His lips tightened into a line and he nodded once, curtly, before stepping back and letting Ophelia stand in front of him to face the gathering.

Titus, Maiwenn, and Ewan moved away, whispering among themselves, their gazes tied to Ophelia.

Ophelia folded the parchment and tucked it inside the pocket of her vest. She raised her arms to call for attention. Conversation halted and everyone—riders, squires, and castle staff—stilled and went silent. The only sounds were the distant growls and mewling of young dragons that carried on the wind from the stables.

"We will mourn my great father at dawn," she said, her voice nearly as powerful as Marius's. "Mist Knights, I am your new commander."

A shiver ran down Tahlia's back and she gripped her sword's hilt. This was the worst outcome possible.

"Surely this is a mistake," Tahlia whispered to Fara. "Marius should be next in line."

Fara's gaze cut to the knights around them and she took Tahlia's hand in the way she did when she wanted Tahlia to hush.

"Meet at the southern barbican one hour before dawn, Mist Knights. Wear your best. My father deserves your respect."

The knights raised whatever weapons they had on hand. Bows, daggers, and swords were lifted high and shouts went up. "Hail, Commander Gaius! Hail, Commander Ophelia!"

Tahlia unsheathed her gladius and joined in belatedly, sweat beading along her upper lip. With Ophelia in charge, she would have to be very careful about talking to Marius concerning Ophelia's presence earlier in the commander's chambers.

When the chant died down, Tahlia dragged Fara beyond the courtyard and into the arena.

"What are you doing? Don't you need to talk to the High Captain?" Fara asked, tugging at Tahlia's hold on her arm.

Once behind the arena wall, Tahlia checked that no one was within earshot and pulled Fara close.

Then she told her everything—about Ophelia sneaking around, about the dagger in her hand, and how it didn't fit with the story of how Ophelia had been barred from Gaius's rooms.

Fara chewed her thumbnail. "If you falsely accuse a commander publicly, you'll be back in front of that death sentence dragon again before you can say 'I'm new here.'"

When Tahlia had first arrived to compete for a place in the order, her half-human blood had set her on a path to death by dragon fire. There was an old Green-flanked Terror whose job it was to end the lives of riders who committed serious crimes. Tahlia shuddered, recalling the dragon's dead eyes. With the help of the king and queen, as well as Marius, Tahlia had barely escaped that fiery fate.

"I'll just tell Marius," Tahlia said. "Do you really think Gaius named his daughter as the next commander?"

"It's an unusual choice, but I suppose it's possible. It would be a tough thing for Ophelia to fake that he had chosen her, seeing as the other captains would have to approve the sealed death document written in Gaius's hand."

There were plenty of ways to deceive without directly lying.

Fara's gaze intensified. "I do not like that look, Tahlia. Seriously, even if they don't put you to death for the accusation, they will banish you from the mountain and you'll be cut off from your dragon."

Tahlia's throat went tight. Separation from the Seabreak would feel akin to losing a limb. No, worse than that. It would be like having her soul scraped out of her body.

Shoving her fear into a dark corner of her mind, Tahlia started to walk away. "I'm going to find him."

Fara stopped her with a hand. "Now?"

Tahlia swallowed. "Yes."

"Be careful," Fara said. "Promise me you won't do anything insane."

"Your definition is different from mine," Tahlia said.

"We are using my definition here."

"I can't always be careful, Fara."

"You are never careful. I'm just asking for you to give it a whirl in this mad situation."

A dark laugh rose from Tahlia. "I'll do what I can."

Fara hugged her close, then released her. "I'm going to eat my way through the market and try to pretend this isn't happening."

"Good plan."

Fara started in the direction of the arena's main entrance, waving a hand in the air as a farewell.

Tahlia knew exactly how lucky she was to have Fara in her life, but Tahlia had to risk telling Marius everything she'd seen. He needed to know. Now.

CHAPTER 9
TAHLIA

The corridors were oddly silent and Tahlia hurried through the passageways toward Marius's chambers, which were situated above the great hall. A stone staircase wound its way up to the next floor of the keep and arrow slits set into the walls let in rectangles of the morning sunlight.

Marius's oaken door boasted a scene that had become familiar. A view one could only see from a dragon's back, the door's carving depicted the keep, the two rings of stone walls that surrounded it, the main waterfall that Tahlia couldn't recall the name of at the moment, and the jagged peaks that ran from Dragon Tail like a dragon's spiny back.

Tahlia lifted the bronze knocker—formed to look like a dragon's tooth—and let it bang down, heralding her arrival.

Marius answered quickly, swinging the door open. His eyes held the darkness of grief, but one corner of his mouth flicked upward as he looked at her. He stole her breath with his rough-edged good looks.

"Lady Tahlia."

His voice was a balm, easing her busy mind and anxious heart.

He stepped back, and she entered his rooms. The scent of beeswax candles and Marius's scent of cloves tickled Tahlia's nose. He offered her a pillowed chair by a small round table that held a decanter of water. She took it and looked up at him.

"I am so sorry about Commander Gaius. He was very important to you."

"To all of us." He poured two cups of water and set one in front of her.

Oh, the way his words broke on the last syllable... Her heart ached for him. "But especially to you, I think."

"It's true." He drank down a swallow and studied her face. "You already know me better than most, my lady."

The sorrow in his eyes pressed against her pulse points, making it hard not to hang her head and weep with him.

Maybe she should, but...

"I have some uncomfortable information," she said, keeping her tone even.

Frowning, he sat in the chair opposite hers. "I'm listening."

"First off, I'm here as your, um, friend, not as your warrior."

"Tahlia, just tell me."

She cleared her throat, hoping this wasn't an incredibly terrible mistake. "Earlier, when we last saw the commander..."

Marius's gaze strayed to a window set high in the wall and his chest moved in a slow, deep breath. "Yes?" Grief shadowed his every small movement.

"I left my gladius at his front door, and when I returned to retrieve it, the door was unlocked."

"But Commander Ophelia stated that it had been locked. Perhaps not yet?"

She held up a hand. "That's not even the strange part. Ophelia was there. In the commander's chambers." Tahlia wasn't ready to call Ophelia by her new title. "She didn't see me, but I watched her leave a back room and head toward the living area with a knife in her hand."

He lifted an eyebrow. "You're certain?"

"I am."

"His death could have been from natural causes, and it could have happened an hour or more after you saw her there."

"What about the knife? And why didn't she come forward when we were there? Also, you would think that Commander Gaius would have spoken more carefully if he'd known she was just in the other room and fully able to hear us talking about her."

"Well, perhaps he thought it wasn't a bad thing to bring up her struggles. Maybe she was ashamed of having her father protect her in the way he did, by asking us to refrain from courting."

"And the knife?"

"Ophelia is never long without a blade to toy with.

She is always flipping one or fiddling with the hilt of the Laqqaran dagger she wears at her belt."

Tahlia hadn't noticed that, but, of course, she had only met Ophelia fourteen days or so ago. Besides that, Tahlia's focus had been on Marius more than anyone else.

"Will you question her about it?" she asked.

Marius stilled, his gaze going oddly vacant. His body appeared frozen; he wasn't even breathing. Just sitting there, staring at nothing.

"Marius?"

No response. Her heart gave a heavy thump. She stood, leaning over the table, and knocked over her cup of water. Ignoring the pooling liquid, she reached for his hand.

He rose quickly and he blinked at her like he was just waking up.

What in the name of the Old Ones was happening here? "Marius, what is wrong? Are you feeling all right?"

"I..." He rubbed a hand over his face as water dripped from the table onto the wooden floorboards. "I think so, but..."

Tahlia came around the table to stand in front of him and reached for him again. His arm fell to his side and he looked at her wide-eyed.

"You're scaring the hells out of me. What is going on?"

He stepped back, alarm glaring in his eyes. "I can't. I don't." He gritted his teeth and a growl emanated from deep in his throat.

"Did I upset you? Is this about Gaius? Should I call a Healer?"

Breathing out slowly, he shut his eyes then opened them again. "Tahlia." His voice was low and his words cracked here and there. "I need you to leave."

"What? But—"

"Go."

The command hit her like a kick to the heart. "I will, of course, but you're worrying me."

"Now, Tahlia. Leave." His lips tilted downward, and he fisted his hands at his sides. "I'm sorry."

He was torn. But about what?

Tahlia held out her hands. "All right. I'm leaving. Just promise to send for me, or anyone, if you want to talk. It's fine to show emotion even if you are High Captain, you know. But you want to be alone. I understand that." She gave him what she hoped was a supportive smile.

She walked backward out of the chamber and he shut the door without another word.

In the corridor under the flickering sconces, she stared at the door's carvings as her pulse pounded and her chest ached with the hurt of his rejection.

Was he trying to create distance between them emotionally to honor Gaius's last request—to stay apart until Ophelia was steadier? But the way he'd gone so still... Was it grief? It could shake a person and turn them inside out, certainly. Still pondering, she turned and started down the winding stairs, heading for the quiet wooded spot just behind the keep. She needed to think.

That had to be it—grief had him acting mad. Understandable. Time would help, and she'd give him all the space he required. He deserved to be supported in whatever way helped best, and she'd make sure he received that support. Even if Ophelia was up to no good...

CHAPTER 10
TAHLIA

That evening, the great hall's massive hearth snapped and crackled with flames as servers distributed pancakes fried with honey and sesame seeds, freshly steamed mussels from the river covered in a fermented fish sauce, the pale cheese common in the Shrouded Mountains, and, of course, bread.

Fara was annihilating an entire loaf on her own when Tahlia found her at a seat near the fire.

Tahlia leaned toward Fara and raised an eyebrow. "I can come back if you two need a little alone time."

Fara gave her a withering look. "You riders are mad for getting on the backs of dragons, but I will say, the bakers up here are far more talented than the ones in the valley."

Accepting a plate from one of the servers, Tahlia had a seat beside Fara. The mussels were hot and the sauce was strange but deliciously biting. She enjoyed half a pancake, then washed it down with watered crystal wine.

"Are you going to eat that?" Fara pointed to the other half of the pancake.

"No, please take it. I don't want you nibbling on my fingers if you get hungry at midnight."

"Where have you been all day? How did it go with the High Captain?" Fara glanced at the two squires sitting opposite them, but Tahlia didn't think they were too concerned about anything Fara and Tahlia might discuss. They seemed fully engrossed in their small game of three dice.

"I needed some time to ponder." She'd spent hours walking the trails that branched from the keep and out of the walls to the pine forest surrounding the castle grounds.

"Whoa, I haven't heard that one from you before. This must be pretty bad."

"Well, Marius is definitely struggling with the death," Tahlia said, keeping her voice to a whisper.

Fara nodded. "But did he listen to your, um, to your information?"

"He did, but he wasn't himself. I'll have to talk to him again later. Maybe after the funeral and a few days to get his head on straight."

"Might take longer."

"It might, but I think he needs some space right now."

Fara licked her fingers. "My parents would have died seeing me do this. I am really starting to enjoy life up here in the peaks."

Tahlia patted Fara's shoulder. "I'm glad. I would hate to be up here without you."

Tahlia tried to eat more and push her worry aside while Fara feasted, but Marius's stony face kept flashing through her mind's eye. She tapped Fara with an elbow. Fara lowered a large wooden spoon of honeyed oats and glanced Tahlia's way.

"Yes?"

"Sorry to disturb you and your next true love, but I'm going to the stables. I just want to check on the Seabreak."

"Want me to come?" Fara asked. "I can apply that salve to her left wing again if you think we should." She set her spoon down and wiped her mouth on one of the linen napkins folded at each place setting.

"No, I'd rather go on my own."

Fara smiled and went back to her oatmeal. "Don't get lost."

"I haven't yet."

"Those stables are wild. You could walk around in the passageways for ten years without finding an end."

"You'd probably get roasted before a decade passed," Tahlia said, trying for a lighter tone.

"Most likely." Fara snickered. But she snagged Tahlia's sleeve before she could leave. "Seriously though, watch out for..." She glanced around them. "For that one person."

She meant Ophelia. "I will."

This wasn't a ridiculous warning like many of Fara's cautionary comments. If Marius decided to tell Ophelia that Tahlia had seen her, even if he intended no harm,

Ophelia would go after Tahlia. Who would everyone believe was at fault if she and Ophelia ended up in a fight? Their new commander, that was who. They'd have no choice.

No one—save Marius—would risk their bonded dragon for Tahlia. She was too new. She didn't even blame them. No, she had to find proof that Ophelia was involved in her father's death.

Had she killed him? Did Tahlia really think that of the female?

She chewed the inside of her cheek as she slipped from the great hall into the foyer, heading for Ophelia's chambers. She didn't like fibbing to Fara, but she didn't want her worrying.

Stars sparkled across the stained glass of the windows and reflected off the crystals embedded in the stone walls. She crossed the foyer and started up the side stairs.

Had Ophelia killed Gaius? Maybe. Who else had access to him? The other knights and Remus. But this was Ophelia. Evil Ophelia. Yeah, she was the best bet. Before she could repeat that thought to anyone, she had to find proof.

She hid in the darkness at the edge of the corridor that split off toward the bedchambers, the kitchens, and the various meeting halls. Riders and staff passed by, most of them solemn and quiet due to Commander Gaius's death. Once the area was empty of people, Tahlia slipped down the hallway that led to Ophelia's rooms.

The sconces' yellow light drew Tahlia around a tight corner, up another set of stairs, and past a new tapestry showing the wedding of Queen Revna and King Lysanael. The Unseelie King had been stitched into the scene even though everyone knew the two males hadn't made peace until well after the pictured event. Unseelie monsters' eyes glittered with gold thread, and the Unseelie King's skin was shown to be a deep gray with a scattering of dragon scales here and there. Tahlia shivered and kept on. Riding dragons was glorious, but being a dragon shifter? That would be madness.

Ophelia's door, another oaken beast of a thing, was carved with swirls of clouds and stars. Tahlia leaned against the wood to listen. If she was found, what would she say? Perhaps something about condolences. Yes, that would work well enough.

Footsteps sounded down the corridor, and Tahlia's heart shot into her throat. She lunged for the opposite side of the hallway and concealed herself behind a row of hooks and hanging cloaks. Ophelia approached, her mouth bunched and her brow furrowed. She removed a key from her belt and unlocked her door.

Once Ophelia disappeared, Tahlia moved to follow.

Thankfully, Ophelia hadn't locked the door from the inside and the oaken entrance swung open with a creak. Tahlia froze, waiting, hoping she hadn't been heard. The smell of the apartments was odd. Smoke, but not regular candle smoke. This scent was harsher. Hiding under that, a sickly odor hung in the air. Illness? Rot? Mold?

A bang and a shuffle indicated that Ophelia had gone farther in and was moving something large and heavy across the floor.

Tahlia dared to lean around the corner of the entryway. Ophelia's back was to her. She was kneeling and dragging a rectangular carpet into what seemed to be a random spot in the middle of the living area.

Ophelia paused in her redecorating mission and started to peer over her shoulder. Tahlia ducked back and held her breath.

"Lue, is that you?"

Lue was Ophelia's squire.

Sweat rolled down the back of Tahlia's neck.

The sound of Ophelia's boots and the splash of water from farther away let Tahlia relax. She peeked around the entryway wall again and saw Ophelia at a wash basin near a round window. She was cleaning her hands. Tahlia caught a flash of the back of Ophelia's left hand. A slash of gray-black charring showed.

If Ophelia was expecting Lue soon, Tahlia needed to go. She turned to leave, cracking the door open a bit more. Keeping every movement slow and sure, Tahlia made her way into the corridor, then she scurried back the way she'd come.

The sconce near the corridor's tight turn had flickered out. Tahlia ran straight into something.

"I knew it, you little beast," Fara whispered. "Let's get out of here while we're still breathing."

Tahlia rubbed her shoulder where the buckle of Fara's side-swept half-cloak had hit her. "What do you mean?"

"I knew you weren't off to the stables. You don't possess the ability to stay out of harm's way."

"This hallway is safer than a labyrinth cave system full of dragons."

Fara glanced at Tahlia, frowning as she walked on. "Ophelia is the worst kind of monster."

"You're not wrong. But I did see some odd things."

"Like what?" Fara asked.

Tahlia hurried down the stairs with Fara at her side. The sound of conversations trickled up from the foyer.

"The person in question was moving a rug."

Fara faked a shiver. "Horrifying."

Tahlia smacked Fara's arm with the back of her hand. "The place smelled so strange. Like someone had been sick there for a long time. And the chamber smelled like smoke."

"Just because Ophelia has an ague," Fara whispered as they crossed the foyer to return to the great hall, "keeps too many candles lit, and enjoys redecorating doesn't mean she murdered her father. Although I'm here for throwing insults her way regardless. Just not out loud."

Tahlia eyed the crowd in the hall, searching for a certain grouchy High Captain. "Something is off here. I just know it."

Fara reached for the milk and egg puddings sitting in a tidy row on a sideboard. "Well, for now, it's nothing a tiropatina with pomegranate seeds won't fix."

The desserts were fantastic and no one bothered them when they retired to bed, but Tahlia didn't sleep a wink. She hadn't seen Marius the rest of the evening and she could not shake the feeling that she should be working harder to uncover what in the hells was going on.

CHAPTER II
TAHLIA

At the front of a mile-and-a-half-long line of townsfolk, the Order of the Mist Knights donned full regalia for the funeral and Blessing Procession. The sky still hadn't fulfilled its promise of a storm, but the clouds shifted and curled above the knights. Tahlia hadn't earned any purple tassels for her white riding leathers yet, but she was given a circle of golden laurels like all the other knights. They stood side by side with their squires adorned in dark blue across from them. Tahlia had filed in behind Titus and Ewan, hoping that she'd get a chance to check on Marius with a private whisper, but he had arrived later than the rest and had taken a spot at the very front of the line.

Marius had been late. Marius. The male who had his own water clock, custom-made in the valley and probably worth a small fortune, on his bedside table. The male who was always fifteen minutes early to training sessions and who arrived a half hour before mission takeoffs.

She leaned forward to peer at him. He glanced her way, making her heart triple-beat like she was some lovesick adolescent. Dark circles hung below his stormy eyes and he drew back his lips, showing his full Fae fangs as he looked her way. He wasn't angry but frustrated for some unknown reason. He seemed insistent on gaining her notice. She would be sure to grab him after this was over and see what was going through his mind.

The heralds' trumpets sounded and Marius straightened. The other knights blocked the view of him, so she stood at attention too, ready to give respect to Gaius.

A masked male wearing Gaius's livery drove a gilded cart with the casket lying in the back. Black roses, snowy mistbloom, and the commander's golden laurel circlet sat atop the casket. Tahlia's heart cinched as the casket passed slowly in front of them. Gaius could have further fought her presence in the order, but he had accepted her at the queen's behest. Since entering the order officially, Tahlia had never been treated as less by him. He had been a good male, a great rider, and a strong leader. She truly wished he would have an afterlife fit for the Old Ones.

The trumpeting stopped and all turned toward the Tombcarver, who had obviously been at work since the announcement of Gaius's death. The Tombcarver stood in front of the death monument and read aloud the words he'd carved.

"Commander Gaius Maximus Aeneas, defender of

the Realm of Lights and son of the mountain. In death as in life, may you conquer evil and hear your name echoed in the clouds."

The knights knelt, Tahlia following as best she could, then they scooped a handful of the churned dirt beside the cobblestones of the road. She had been wondering why there was a row of earth piled along the pathway. The knights set their handfuls of dirt against their chests and spoke the commander's name as one.

"Gaius, we mourn you."

Tahlia hadn't been taught the funeral process, so she was late to speak and kept her voice as solemn as possible. She glanced at Marius. Unshed tears glimmered in his eyes and her heart broke for him. She longed to pull him into her arms and let him tell her all the stories about the man who had been a father figure to him for so many years.

The rest of the day passed in a quiet blur of conversations with Maiwenn, Fara, Titus, and Enora. At sunset, Tahlia and Fara went to the stables to check the Seabreak's wing. She'd injured it two days ago. Nothing serious, and the injury hadn't hindered her flying, but Tahlia wanted to keep it that way by consistently salving the area and making certain the dragon stretched that wing to keep it from going stiff.

The Seabreak's head emerged from the cave-like stall as Tahlia and Fara approached. The dragon blinked her glittering eyes and let out a puff of black smoke. Joy lifted Tahlia's heart at the sight, a sensation she always had in the presence of...

A name rang like a gentle bell in her head and shivers danced down her spine.

Vodolija.

"What's wrong?" Fara asked.

Tahlia reached out to smooth the top of the Seabreak's cyan-blue snout. "Vodolija?"

The dragon met her gaze and dipped her head. Tahlia's heart squeezed and she coughed, grasping at her vest. But the feeling subsided, and, oddly energized, she took a deep breath.

Vodolija stared at Tahlia, and together, their souls sang with victory.

The bond was complete.

Tahlia grinned and pressed herself against the dragon.

Fara whooped and raised a fist. "You found her name! The bond is whole!"

"I heard it in my head like she spoke it to me."

Wonder hung on Tahlia like a second cloak. She took a plain pancake from her pocket and fed it to Vodolija. The dragon nibbled the treat, then licked Tahlia's palm for the crumbs.

"I have no idea if there is a meaning behind it," Tahlia said.

Fara hummed and tapped her pointy chin. "It sounds like a northern coastal name."

"Agreed. I'll ask Marius about it." A weight settled on Tahlia's chest.

Like he'd been summoned, the High Captain himself strode by and made her breath catch in her throat.

"High Captain!" Tahlia raised a hand, hoping he would act like his normal grouchy, stern self. She wished for that odd mood he'd been in to be gone.

Marius turned, his face only partially illuminated by the one sconce on the wall. His gaze was pinched and his lips moved like he was about to utter something important, but he just bowed his head briefly and greeted them. "Lady Tahlia. Lady Fara."

Fara headed into the stall. "I'll see to Vodolija's wing."

Tahlia stepped closer to Marius. "Are you all right?" He looked like he'd had two pounds of goblinbloom shoved down his gorgeous throat. "I'm here if you want to talk. Or to fly. We could just go for a bit and clear our heads?"

His eyes shut for a second. "I can't. I have... I must leave."

"Leave? Where to?"

"A personal mission."

"I'd be happy to come along."

"I wish that I could welcome you, but I can't."

He extended his hand, then recoiled in the same way he had before. What was going on with him? Was he angry with her in addition to feeling grief?

She looked left and right to be certain they were alone. "Marius, you can tell me anything. And if you want space, I'm completely fine with that. Just talk to me. You are hard to read on a good day. Now it's like the greatest mystery in all the realms just trying to figure you out."

"I'm sorry. I just can't." His throat moved in a disjointed swallow like he was holding back an unnamed emotion. "Stay here. Please keep this mission secret."

An invisible fist gripped Tahlia's heart and squeezed it mercilessly. The poor bastard. Gods, she wished she could fix this somehow. Make him laugh. Or at least give even a flicker of hope in his dreamy-as-hells eyes. "But, Marius, if you need help in some way..."

His eyes grew hazy and he turned his head, facing the wall to the side and behind her. He rubbed the back of his neck and cleared his throat, his focus then returning to her. "Keep on flying. You will be a legend someday."

She opened her mouth to say something, anything, but he quickly walked away into the dimly lit corridor, presumably heading for Ragewing.

Fara peeked her head out of the stall. "What was that all about?"

"Marius had tears in his eyes."

"Poor fellow. He really cared for the commander."

"Yes. It was so sudden."

"There's a *but* in your tone."

Tahlia chewed her lip. "He isn't acting like he's just grieving. He said he has a personal mission to go on."

"Right now?" Fara frowned.

"I think so. That's odd, isn't it?"

"It's not out of the question," Fara said, "but the timing is strange."

Tahlia shrugged. "Perhaps Ophelia is ordering him to go somewhere, some last request of her father's?"

Fara's eyes narrowed. "Or she is pretending it is."

"I'm going to follow him." Tahlia entered the stall

and patted Vodolija, indicating she should move closer to the saddle that sat on the narrow wooden shelf embedded in the stone wall. "Such a gorgeous lady," she murmured to the dragon. She dropped a quick kiss on one of her shiny, shiny scales.

"Will you ask your unit to join you?"

"No, why?"

"Because they are your unit. Your loyalty to one another is tighter than family."

"They don't trust me enough just to go along. They'd ask questions I don't have answers to. Besides, what about all your warnings?"

Tahlia's heart ached painfully at the thought of losing Vodolija. She ran a hand down the dragon's scales and breathed in slowly, just enjoying being in the dragon's calming presence.

"I meant that it could be deadly to accuse Ophelia in front of the other units, the staff, Bloodworkers, or Healers. Your unit isn't going to report you." Fara looked at Tahlia like the very idea was unthinkable.

"You didn't see Claudia and Justus at the tavern. They don't like me. At all. Claudia is tight with Maiwenn, who as we both know loathes everything about me."

"Why didn't you tell me more about that night? I'm here for you, Tahl."

Fara's eyes had softened, and Tahlia's spirit railed against the pity in their depths. Maybe it wasn't pity, but it sure felt like it.

"Because honestly, I don't love whining about people not liking me. It makes me feel... I don't know, Fara."

"It makes you feel weak and you hate that."

"Wow. Yes, fine. It does."

"But just because you feel that way doesn't make it true. You aren't weak because you care about what they think. Being upset about the time they're taking to trust you doesn't make you lesser."

Tahlia's skin itched and she wanted this conversation to end already. "Well, regardless, I can't risk it."

"You have to face them, Tahlia. I'll beat them into a pile of broken bones with nothing but my indomitable rage, then they'll have no choice but to listen."

A low laugh tripped from Tahlia, and Fara scowled.

"But seriously, if you're ever to build that trust," Fara said, "you need to lean into them and tell them the truth. I am the danger alarm between us, remember? So if I'm telling you it's safe to talk to them, it must be, right?"

"Maybe if we'd been flying together for longer than a handful of days, yes. But now? Not a chance. I'm not wasting time arguing when I can just go and figure it out myself."

Fara helped Tahlia maneuver the saddle onto the dragon's back. Order saddles differed from horse saddles in that they had an extra seat behind the main one. Riders could take on injured folk or fellow riders whose dragon had been incapacitated. Sometimes riders used the additional spot for a bedroll or bag. Also, dragon saddles didn't have large pommels and were fairly low profile.

"Well, then, stubborn face, I'm going with you," Fara said.

"What?" Tahlia never thought she'd see the day Fara

wanted to ride a dragon. "You can't do that and you know it. Squires don't ride dragons."

"They do in some instances." Fara glanced at the Seabreak, her eyes a little too wide for the confidence she was pretending to have. Tahlia knew well how scared Fara was of flying on dragonback.

Tahlia squinted at her. "You actually want to ride Vodolija?"

"No. Not even a little bit," Fara said.

The dragon twisted and eyed Fara cooly. Fara gave her a nervous smile, all teeth and Fae fangs.

"But if she'll allow it, I'm riding along." Fara straightened and put her hands on her hips. "As a proper friend, I can't let you head off into who knows where on your own, following a scary male who doesn't want you there."

Tahlia's heart turned to pudding. "Aww. You are the dearest friend." She hurried over and gave her a quick hug before going back to helping Vodolija slide on her bridle. "But Fara, Marius isn't going to hurt me."

"Normally, no. But he's acting off."

"He is. He heard me use Vodolija's name, but he didn't even mention it. We've been talking about Vodolija and my bond with her a good bit, so that seems like strange behavior." A shiver of said bond link traveled from Tahlia's heart and branched into her arms, a delightful sensation.

Vodolija nickered and eased herself against Tahlia gently.

"If he's being different than he has been the entire time you've been here, then you have no idea what's really going on," Fara said. "It could be one of a million horrid things! I can at least watch your back and give you some rest at night to sleep. Or whatever. Squire things like that."

Tahlia chuckled. "Squire things. Right. Well, Vodolija might not want you on her back. What do you say, my friend?" she asked the dragon.

Vodolija lifted her head and jerked it down again.

"Wow, all right. She says yes," Tahlia said, giving Fara a wide-eyed look. "You're certain about this?"

Fara grimaced. "No, but also yes."

"What about the million things that could go wrong?"

"There always are that many, really. Another day, another potential moment to die in a flurry of mistakes." Fara shrugged.

"That's the most Fara response in the world."

"Thank you."

Tahlia shook her head as they used the rope to fasten the girth under Vodolija's belly. Fara put out the stall's one torchlight, then they waited, still and quiet in the dark stall, until Marius and Ragewing passed by.

As they followed in Marius's footsteps and left the stables, the sky dimmed, clouds wrapping the stars and moon in black. The scent of rain blew past Tahlia's face. Ragewing was a slash of movement far above Dragon Tail peak.

"We have to move now, or we'll lose them."

Vodolija bent low and allowed them both to mount, Fara sitting behind Tahlia. Fara's whispered curses weren't exactly calming Tahlia's already frazzled nerves.

She'd only escaped punishment by dragon fire a handful of days ago, and here she was, breaking yet another rule, ignoring a direct order.

The Seabreak coursed into the sky and Tahlia prayed to the Old Ones that she wasn't making the biggest mistake of her life.

CHAPTER 12
TAHLIA

"This is officially the worst idea you've ever had," Fara shouted over the pelting rain and thunder.

Tahlia glared over her shoulder. "I told you not to come. This is your idea. Not mine."

Fara buried her head between Tahlia's shoulder blades, which was comical because Tahlia was so much smaller than Fara. "I couldn't let you go alone. You know that!"

"Yes, you could have."

Fara began to argue again, but lightning cracked, and she screamed instead of finishing her sentence.

"Stop digging your fingers into my sides," Tahlia said, turning so Fara might hear over the storm.

"It can't hurt you. You're wearing leathers!"

"Your fingers are worse than arrows. Stop it!"

Fara detached her vicious grip, then wrapped her entire arms around Tahlia's middle. A breath gusted from Tahlia.

"I need to breathe to get us there alive, Fara."

"I'm going to kill Marius. I'm going to strangle him until he is dead and then kick him after."

"That's ridiculous," Tahlia said, the wind biting her cheeks and eyes. She was soaked through and shivering.

"He deserves it for dragging us into this mess."

"No, it's ridiculous that you think you can kill him."

"Shut it, Tahl. Seriously!" Fara groaned as another round of thunder started up.

The storm eventually relented, and the sun pierced the blanket of cloud cover, but there was no sign of Marius or Ragewing. Tahlia had completely lost them in the dark and driving rain.

"What are we going to do? Can Vodolija scent Ragewing at all?"

"I think she still has an idea of where they are because she feels sure of herself and isn't trying to land." Being bonded to a dragon was amazing…and mysterious. Tahlia wasn't certain how she knew what Vodolija was thinking, but somehow she had a sense of it.

They flew on, the sun drying them out nicely as the wind finished the job. Only stopping twice for Vodolija to drink from the river and for a bite to eat, they covered a lot of ground.

As they rose into the air, letting Vodolija's better vision spot and trail Ragewing and Marius, Fara made a growling sort of grumble near Tahlia's ear.

"Other than the fact that I'm completely disobeying a direct order, what is bothering you?" Tahlia asked.

"If I had to guess, we are almost to the Kingdom of Spirits," Fara answered.

A chill rolled through Tahlia. No one dared to enter the lost kingdom. Old tales of vicious spirits and dangerous ghosts had given the land its name.

"I read about a rare plant that only grows in this area. It has blood-colored leaves and was used ages ago to help Fae bond with dragons."

Tahlia wanted to listen to her, but there was too much at risk to have a chat about plants.

"Would we even be able to cross the border of this ghostly place?" Tahlia asked.

There was one story Tahlia had heard at a tavern that involved some magical barrier between the Kingdom of Spirits and the rest of the Realm of Lights. Technically, the lost kingdom remained part of the Seelie Fae kingdom and under King Lysanael and Queen Revna's rule. It existed within the Veil. But no one went in and came back to tell new tales.

"I hope not. It would be madness to try. Why would Marius even want to enter? Surely Ragewing won't allow it. Dragons are many things, but stupid isn't one of them."

Vodolija growled, her body rumbling under Tahlia.

The Kingdom of Spirits. What could be in that area that involved the order?

THAT EVENING, moonlit mist billowed around Vodolija's wings, the thick gray blocking everything except a strange distant light on the ground below. It shimmered like a ghostly gold version of those phosphorescent larvae that glowed in the creek during summers at home.

It was definitely creepy, but shivers of excitement ran down Tahlia's back. She hadn't joined the order for easy days in the sun. She'd risked all to experience this type of adventure.

"I hope you can tell where they are," Tahlia said to Vodolija, leaning over a bit as Fara hissed prayers that might have been less prayish and more curseish to every Old One and god she could think of. "Because I have no clue."

Fara sighed. "Please just lie to me and say everything will be fine."

Vodolija tossed her head and flew onward, showing confidence. Not that dragons ever deigned to show humility or ever admitted when they were wrong.

Tahlia grinned over her shoulder. "I think that's what the head toss means."

Fara rolled her eyes. "She could be saying she is about to dump us and go home."

Tahlia laughed even though fatigue pulled at her. It had been a very long day.

The cold air bit at Tahlia's cheeks. The temperature had dropped since sundown. She lifted the cowl she wore over her leathers and fastened her cloak's three extra clasps, drawing the wool tightly around her chest and shoulders. Fara gave her a hand and offered a pair of leather gloves. Tahlia accepted them gratefully and held the reins in her teeth as she tugged them on. Fara cursed the entire time.

Vodolija dove suddenly, Tahlia sucked a breath, and Fara shrieked.

Wings spread wide, the dragon soared toward the

ground or whatever was below. The mist and the night continued to hinder Tahlia's view. Would they be far enough behind Marius and Ragewing to keep their presence a secret? If the wind blew the other direction, Ragewing would surely scent Vodolija. Tahlia gripped the saddle's pommel and tightened the muscles in her legs and stomach to prepare for a rough landing. The Seabreak hit the ground even harder than Tahlia had guessed she would and she nearly lost her seat. Fara did. She went tumbling over a wing and landed with a wet smack on the ground.

"Fara! Are you all right?" Tahlia hissed in a whisper as she dismounted.

Fara's chest moved in three quick breaths, then one steadier one. "Yes, I'm well. Thank you so much. Please remind me to absolutely never, ever get on a dragon again. That experience will fill my nightmares until the end of my days." She cursed creatively. "I forgot about the ride home. Kill me."

Ignoring Fara now that she knew she was well enough to whine, Tahlia squinted into the distance.

Beyond two dark hills, a large shape and a smaller one walked side by side toward that glowing light. It was Ragewing and Marius. Had to be, right?

Tahlia untied her bow and full quiver from the back of the saddle, her boots squelching in the mud. "Let's go."

Fara got up and straightened her belt and dagger. "Lead on."

Tahlia strapped the quiver of blue-fletched arrows to her back and started forward, Vodolija beside her with scaled head low and wings tucked. Tahlia nocked an arrow just in case it wasn't Marius and Ragewing, but the closer they got, the more sure she was about her guess.

Fara was pale, or as pale as someone with purple skin could be, and she was too quiet.

"Please whisper a warning of impending doom now and then so I know you're all right," Tahlia said quietly.

"We will all leave here with foot rot."

"There's the Fara I know and love."

What would Marius do if he saw her here? Would he demand she return? Probably. Would she follow that order? She'd pretend to, but no. Marius wasn't like this, someone who just flew off recklessly into dangerous scenarios. He thought things out. He made plans and followed the rules. This secret trip to a region known for its deadly spirits made no sense whatsoever. Marius had lost his handsome mind and Tahlia was going to get to the bottom of this. Besides, she wouldn't abandon him here. Even with Ragewing, the spirits in this forlorn kingdom of old might be too much for him. She wasn't going to leave him just to follow his rules or anyone else's. If she managed to save Marius or solve this problem he was having, it would be worth the consequences.

Vodolija, Fara, and Tahlia walked between the two hills. Marius and Ragewing stood at the bottom of a slope. A break of rowans hid most of Ragewing; only his head stood out above one of the smaller trees.

Like the gruesome teeth of a buried giant, five standing stones set into a rough circle marked the entry to the kingdom. Even though the Kingdom of Spirits was technically in the Realm of Lights and held by King Lysanael and Queen Revna, the old boundary markers had been left in place for safety. No one wanted to stumble into this haunted place. Well, no one but Tahlia's possibly less-than-wise adventurous side.

So for the thousandth time, Tahlia wondered why in the name of all that was holy Marius, a notorious by-the-book type, was calmly strolling up like he'd been planning this reckless excursion for ages.

Ragewing and Marius passed by the standing stones and the mist spun around them, hiding them completely.

"Come on, Vodolija. It'll do no good to sit here and chew our nails over the HC."

Vodolija bunched the scales that served as her eyebrows and huffed smoke into Tahlia's face.

"Okay, maybe you aren't chewing nails, but I do not like how he is acting. I really, really don't."

"That makes two of us," Fara said.

As they made their way to the standing stones, a sound rose on the breeze.

CHAPTER 13
TAHLIA

Fara grabbed Tahlia's sleeve. "No. Nooooo. Please make it stop, Tahlia."

As they walked between the standing stones, the sound increased in volume, the noise a humming or howling... The notes nearly melded into a dark melody, but just when the sound started to follow a pattern, it broke apart like a dropped glass.

The stones' presence weighed on her—in the way an Unseelie monster's energy pressed on a Seelie. It felt like the whole area had eyes and the kingdom was watching her.

"Maybe the stones have some old magic still spilling from them?" Tahlia asked in a whisper.

Vodolija growled quietly, indicating she wasn't thrilled by the feel of the stones either.

"Walk faster." Fara sped up, hurrying out of the stone circle and into the Kingdom of Spirits.

The mist split as they entered the kingdom. Mountains tore at low clouds, snow highlighted sharp peaks, and complete darkness indicated deep crevasses. No bats squeaked, no birds chirruped to announce the approaching dawn, and not even the sound of flowing water or the smallest of creatures rummaging through the scrub broke the eerie quiet. Even as the light paled their surroundings, the ground remained black. A slick mud covered most of the area with thick patches of moss-like islands in the morass.

Fara whimpered and held up her fists like she would hit her way out of this.

"I don't think you can punch ghosts, Fara."

The silver stars bled into the milk-white of dawn. The humming and howling finally faded away.

"I can try."

Shaking her head at Fara, Tahlia squinted to see Marius and Ragewing. They wound through a stretch of flat land. Tahlia, Vodolija, and Fara wouldn't be able to keep their presence a secret for long; there weren't any trees for cover anywhere nearby, and the new day exposed their position.

What was she going to say to Marius? She had to get him to talk, to tell her what he felt about everything—them, the commander, the order. She had to crack him open and get him to spill his secrets. Maybe it was presumptuous to think she was the one who could help him, but the way he'd distanced himself so suddenly pointed to a connection between whatever was making him act oddly and their relationship. Yes, their relationship, or the lack thereof, was involved somehow. She just knew it.

Tahlia, Vodolija, and Fara journeyed on, stopping

now and then to nibble on the bread and dried meat Fara had brought along. Tahlia had a waterskin, which she shared with Vodolija, but they would have to find more water for the dragon or she'd begin to suffer from dehydration. Dragons were tough, but two days of no water would be detrimental. Tahlia was glad she and Vodolija had trained hard with the order and toughened up over the last two weeks, because this place pulled the energy from her limbs. It was likely doing the same to the dragons.

"Do you feel more tired than you should be?" Tahlia asked Fara as she packed away the remnants of their latest snack.

"Definitely. I'm being slowly drained like I'm the skin of water and there's this invisible giant who—" Her words fell away and her arms, which she'd stretched out to demonstrate the size of the giant, dropped as she looked at Tahlia.

Tahlia shook from restrained laughter as Fara glared.

Fara swore and made a rude gesture with her hand. "Screw you, Tahlia."

"I love you, friend."

Fara growled. "Yes, yes. Sure." She tromped off, muttering about death and revenge.

Tahlia went to Vodolija's head and patted her snout gently. The dragon blinked at her like a big cat and tilted her head, the spiraling horns there barely missing Tahlia's face. She smiled and kissed Vodolija's cheek.

Fara was walking backward slowly, eyeing them. "Did you just kiss a dragon? I had thought I saw you do that out of the corner of my eye earlier, but I thought surely I was mistaken."

Tahlia shrugged. "Doesn't every rider kiss their dragon?"

"Ha. No. I'm going with a firm *no*. They aren't cuddly."

"They can be." Tahlia rubbed her nose against Vodolija's snout. "I think she's tired. Should we find a spot to rest?" Tahlia looked from Vodolija to Fara. "I worry about losing sight of them even though these flatlands appear to go on for miles more."

Vodolija started forward, gently bumping Tahlia and letting her know she didn't need a rest.

"I guess not." Tahlia shrugged and followed Fara, Vodolija stepping slow and steady beside her.

They continued on for hours. Time moved differently here as if

Night unfurled over the kingdom, blanketing them in silver starlight and shadows blacker than the darkest paint. It was as if the dark here drew in the light, allowing no starlight to penetrate its depths. The sounds began again, a low howl, then a hum of what sounded like a chorus of people. The hairs on her arms rose. But even though it was terrifying, this kingdom was incredibly interesting and the furthest thing from boring.

Vodolija bumped her roughly and nodded toward her own back. She wanted Tahlia to mount up.

Tahlia waved Fara over and they did as suggested. Relief coursed over Tahlia the second she hit the saddle. They could be airborne in moments if that howling turned into a real threat.

The scent of steel and rain wafted through the air, and Vodolija's head whipped to the side. Tahlia unsheathed her dagger, her heartbeat speeding up. Past a bush heavy with faeberries, a shimmering golden light blurred and wavered.

"What was that?" Fara tightened her hold around Tahlia's waist.

Grunting, Tahlia gripped her dagger and leaned forward in the saddle, squinting to see the anomaly better, but it was only a smear of inconsistent light. Vodolija growled, the sound vibrating through Tahlia.

"Hold, darling. Wait."

The light went out. The scent of metal and ozone immediately disappeared.

Vodolija shook like she wanted to rid herself of the whole experience, then she launched into the sky before Tahlia could order her not to. Fara let out one shriek as they flew into the starlight, the dark below like an ocean teeming with monsters.

"We have to go back home," Fara shouted over the wind.

"We can't. You made your decision to come. I'm not leaving Marius."

"He's very big. Whatever in the hells that was, well, he can handle it."

"You don't know that."

"Do you have any guesses on what made that noise?"

"Ghosts?"

"Please. Let's just go back and you can get all your fellow riders and return and save the day."

"I wish, but that's not how it would go. We left

without permission. We would get kicked out if we were lucky, and Marius would be punished as well. Plus, there's a murderous commander in charge now and she isn't exactly my best friend."

Fara let out various agonized noises and set her head against Tahlia's back. "We are going to die."

"No, we aren't. You will be able to tell your grandchildren about this grand adventure."

"Don't wish children on me! Can you even imagine how worried and protective I'd be about them?"

Tahlia snorted. "They would have no lives at all."

"That's the truth. But they would be alive."

Tahlia chuckled despite the cold fear spreading through her bones.

Whatever had made that noise wanted to be heard. But why? To draw Tahlia, Fara, and Vodolija closer to inspect? To ask for help? They would never know if they didn't land.

"Let's go down, Vodolija," Tahlia said, knowing somehow that the dragon could hear over the wind and understand her. "We have to face this."

The dragon dove and Fara argued the whole way down.

CHAPTER 14
TAHLIA

"I think Vodolija is unhappy. You're asking her to go back to the creepy ghosts," Fara said into Tahlia's ear. "She's diving. Showing aggression. Maybe she wants us off her back so she can go home. I should have stayed home with all that bread. Why am I even here?"

"I might need your fists; plus, who else will make sure I pay attention to every little problem?" Tahlia teased.

If the sound had been a ghost, or ghosts, why had it alerted them like that? Was it curious? Was it even cognizant of its actions? Had it once been a person or was it a creature made of forgotten magic?

There was nothing like this in the rest of the Realm of Lights, certainly. No stories of such spirits except those that came from this broken kingdom, and those tales were sparse and lacking any real information. At least the thing hadn't attacked or injured them. That was a relief.

Perhaps none of the spirits were able to affect the living or had no motivation to do so. But if that were true, then why did border folk often find the bodies of travelers who had ventured too close to this land? The corpses found were described as having skin turned to gold with boils going up and down their arms and not a drop of blood in their bodies. The look of the dead had many proposing the idea that whatever evil had befallen the kingdom had something to do with Mistgold Fae—the families who had ridden dragons for centuries and who had that golden sheen in their blood.

Why did travelers come here anyway? For the same reason Marius had? If so, what was that reason?

They climbed a small rise, then spotted Marius and Ragewing a good ways off, seated at a sparkling fire.

Well, if they could stop for the night, so can we.

"That's bold," Fara said, standing beside Tahlia and gazing down toward the fire. "They're telling everyone they're here. Why isn't Marius more concerned?"

Tahlia shrugged, hiding the bulk of her worry. "Let's keep out of their eyeline."

She led Vodolija back down the rise. Soon enough, the fire Tahlia would make would be visible, but they could remain hidden for a little while longer.

Fara shivered as she helped Tahlia gather fallen limbs and broken sticks from the scattered trees growing here and there. A stretch of dark-leafed trees broadened into a full forest a stone's throw away, and though Tahlia worried about taking on Fara's habit of fearing everything, she wasn't about to go traipsing into the woods. Not after hearing that sound earlier.

Once they had a pile of wood, Vodolija set it ablaze and settled beside it. She trilled with satisfaction, obviously enjoying the heat. Tahlia sat on a small boulder beside Fara and they shivered together.

Fara wiggled her mud-slicked boots. "My feet will never be the same. I'll be tottering around like a hag years before my time. I hope Marius appreciates my hobbling." Her lip curled, showing a fang.

Tahlia removed her riding gloves and held her palms toward the flickering light. Vodolija lifted her head and sniffed the air.

"If you want to hunt," she said to Vodolija. "We're good here. But I do have some dragonbread if you want to stick around…"

The dragon growled low in her throat, and Tahlia chuckled. Vodolija hated that stuff.

Vodolija bowed her head, stood, then walked toward the forest. Tahlia appreciated that she was being careful that her takeoff wouldn't blow out the fire. Vodolija launched into the sky, her sea-hued wings spread as wide as a ship's sails. She was so lovely.

When traveling, the knights always brought dragonbread in case hunting wasn't possible or pickings were slim. A fist-sized serving of dragonbread could sustain a dragon for a full day, sometimes more depending on their activity level and how much they'd eaten recently. The dragons never seemed to savor the special meal, but they ate it when they had to. Marius had said they loathed dragonbread as much as younglings did their daily mineral drink, a supplement that Fae children in the Shrouded Mountains had to imbibe because of the lack of nutrients in their diet during the long winters.

Fara took some dried meat from their bags and heated it over the fire. Tahlia had eaten the stuff during training. It was pretty disgusting, but if you warmed it, it at least felt more like real food. The feeling finally returned to Tahlia's hands and feet as they dined on their meager feast. Tahlia kept an eye on the darkness beyond and the forest. Gods, she was tired, more than she should have been.

The noise of wings had Tahlia on her feet with her bow drawn and an arrow ready in a breath.

Fara had picked up a rock and was poised to throw it.

The shadow above materialized into a dragon Tahlia knew as well as she knew her own.

Ragewing.

The large Heartsworn landed a stone's throw from the fire, and Marius swung out of the saddle and slid to the ground. He looked like a living storm.

Fara sucked a breath through her teeth and took a step back.

Tahlia's heart lurched into her throat. He had a cut along his cheek and the blood there had dried to a dark slash. She longed to touch it, to tend to it, and to ask him how he'd hurt himself. It was so odd to feel like comforting a male who appeared virtually made of solid stone.

Ragewing shook out his scarlet wings, blowing Marius's hair. Marius's gray eyes caught the glimmer of the fire and he fisted his hands as he strode toward Tahlia.

She gave him a wide smile. "Fancy meeting you here."

"Knight, you should not be *here* at all."

Oooh, using his captain voice. "I realize that, but neither should you. In fact, I am pretty sure you disobeyed a direct order."

His nostrils flared and his jaw worked. He looked Tahlia up and down, his gaze like a sweep of his hands. She swallowed and tried not to remember being pressed against this male with nothing between them but desire and joy.

"Lady Tahlia, you will return to the castle. That is an—"

"Hold on." Tahlia returned her arrow to the quiver and set her bow on the ground near the food and supply bags. Then she met his angry gaze. "Look. Hear me out, High Captain. Something is up with you."

"Lady Tahlia..." Fara wrung her hands and looked at Tahlia like she was a madwoman.

Ignoring her for the moment, Tahlia eyed Marius. "If you tell me why you're here, I'll take off. I swear it." She held a fist to her heart. "But I'm not leaving you here where there isn't a single living soul without hearing a solid reason for your little adventure."

"It's none of your concern."

All right, that actually hurt. She fought the urge to press a hand to her stomach. "It is my concern. *You* are my concern."

His eyes bunched at the edges and his throat moved in a swallow. "Tahlia, please. There is something you don't know. I can't..." He broke off, coughing and clearing his throat. When his gaze turned back to her again, he was grimacing as if in pain.

"What is wrong?" She stepped toward him.

He lurched backward and glanced to the side, his lips drawing back like he was in pain. "I am sorry for everything. But you must leave. I can't put you at risk too."

"So you admit you're putting yourself and Ragewing at risk by coming here."

"I'm not an idiot, Tahlia."

Fara snorted. "Could have fooled me," she whispered.

He glared at her and she turned away, suddenly very busy with tidying their supplies.

"It's not exactly a holiday spot," Marius said, a tone of wry humor in his voice.

"Was that an attempt at a joke, High Captain?" Tahlia grinned, thrilled to see him thawing if only for a second.

He rubbed his face with his hands, then dropped them and glanced from Fara to Tahlia. "You will leave once Vodolija returns. That is an order."

"Why?"

Tahlia stepped toward him. He dropped back fast like she was a sword aimed at his jugular. Her heart sputtered. His rejection hurt worse than any damage steel could do.

"I can't..." He growled in a very dragon-like manner and stared at the sky. "I order you to go back to the Shrouded Mountains immediately. To Dragon Tail Peak." His chin dipped down and his eyes found hers. "If you disobey this order, you will be put on probation for a time that I will determine once I return."

"*If* you return. Did you hear that sound earlier? The howling? Do you have any information about it or about this place?" Maybe if she pursued a different line of questioning, he'd give her a clue as to what in every god's name he was up to.

"I saw two spirits when they were singing, for lack of a better word. They mean no harm. Ragewing and I are as safe as we can be considering the scenario."

"What is the scenario exactly?"

His jaw worked, and his teeth clenched. "I..." Shaking his head, he looked at the ground.

"Fine. Don't tell me about your secret mission. Do you actually know you aren't about to be killed by whatever kills everyone that crosses that border or are you just telling me that to get me out of here?"

"I can't lie."

"Oh, right. I tend to forget that because you full Fae are so tricky."

Fara gave Tahlia a narrow-eyed glance.

"This conversation is over," Marius said.

But was it? "Just let me stay one full day. Then I'll go."

"No. Leave. That's an order, Lady Tahlia."

"Marius, I can see the way you're torn. In your eyes, you seem as haunted as this kingdom."

She lifted a hand, longing to stroke the rough line of his jaw, to feel his hot skin under her fingertips. He moved back another step.

Tahlia chewed the inside of her cheek. "Fine," she said, walking away. "If you're going to be ridiculous, I'll just ask the more sensible of you two."

She went to Ragewing and looked up into the dragon's scarlet face.

"Do you think we should be here? Or would you like to grab Marius and fly the hells out immediately before we end up as pale as the blank page, dusted in golden boils, and deposited on some border folk's farm?"

Ragewing's head swiveled and the dragon studied Marius.

"No," Marius said, shaking his head. "We are not leaving."

Ragewing snorted a puff of black smoke and sat back on his haunches.

"You're headed for that glowing light, the shimmering bit of stuff between those mountains, correct?" Tahlia wasn't giving up yet.

"Yes." He shook his head like he had a bug in his ear. "I mean to say, it's none of your concern. Please go."

"Please? But it's an order? Make up your mind, High Captain Marius."

The steel in his eyes hardened and a thrill shot through her at his dangerous beauty, idiot that she was.

"Tahlia." His voice went stony. "You are pushing me to consider punishments I'd rather not order."

"Do tell. What type of punishment is there for a person who saves your life?"

"You are not saving my life."

Fara brought a strip of dried meat to Ragewing, who accepted it with a grunt.

"You don't know that," Tahlia said. "Something haunted and wild could attack you right now and I'd be here, wielding my arrows and—"

"An arrow for the ghost?"

"Can't punch them either from what I hear," Fara mumbled.

Tahlia almost snarled at Marius. "Perhaps my strategy needs amending, but it could happen—I could end up saving your life here, Marius, and wouldn't you look such a fool for wishing me gone?"

"We may be off the books for this journey, but I am still your captain."

She saluted him. "I'm here and ready to obey."

He snorted, the edge of his lips twitching. "You don't even know the meaning of the word."

"I will learn as long as your orders involve me acting on your behalf here in this incredibly lovely disaster you've dragged us into."

"Tahlia, all jesting aside. You truly must—"

Vodolija landed beside Ragewing, cutting off whatever stale warning Marius was about to dole out.

"No deer to be found?" Tahlia asked the Seabreak.

A purring sound stuttered in the back of the dragon's mouth, a noise Tahlia had learned to interpret as pouting.

"Did you find any fresh water?" Tahlia asked Marius.

"Yes. There is a creek not far away. Trees shield it from view, but if you look closely, you'll see it." He glanced at the flames. "We were flying back from it when I spotted your fire."

"Eh, don't look down your nose at me," Tahlia said. "You made a fire too."

"Unlike you, I am experienced. I deal with multiple threats regularly and have done so for years."

"So you're resorting to insults to get me to leave?"

"I'll do whatever it takes," Marius said. "It's not safe for you or Lady Fara to... It's... Tahlia."

He looked ready to explode. What was going on with him?

Holding out her hands, she said softly, "Marius, one day is all I ask. One day, then I leave with no more insults or begging or punishments required."

She longed to make a flirty joke about the punishment, but he had made it clear he wasn't interested in anything like that at the moment. Though it cracked her heart into pieces, she wasn't about to keep pushing him on that front like some jerk with her head up her arse. She only wanted to know why and what was wrong with him. She wasn't sure she could refrain from *all* flirting, but at least she was trying.

"Fine. I give up."

His growl of frustration usually pleased her, but in this case, it only smashed the pieces of her heart into shards that cut her through and through. There was definitely something very wrong with Marius and she was going to figure it out.

CHAPTER 15
MARIUS

He was going to rip a tear in the world. This damned curse was the most frustrating experience he'd ever had. Pacing while Tahlia and Fara built up the fire, he tried to recall deciding to fly here on Ragewing. But there was only the moment with Tahlia in the stables, then... Then nothing. A fog. Darkness where memories should have been.

He went to Ragewing and set his head against the dragon's side. Ragewing blew gently into Marius's hair, tugging it from its leather tie. The warmth of the dragon was more comforting than sitting by the fire with the females. They had arranged two fallen logs near the flickering tinder. But here, with Ragewing, Marius didn't have to look at Tahlia's sweet mouth and pert nose or see the hurt in her dark honey eyes. Ragewing wrapped him in a wing, blocking the restless breeze of this dead kingdom. He could still hear the distant hum and howl of ghosts though. They were in the forest but, thankfully, seemed to be content to remain there. At least, for now.

In the dimness of his wing enclosure, he dragged the tip of his boot in the mud. He was just so tired. Damn Ophelia to the seven hells. Forever. Longer. He was going to strangle the female no matter what the consequences.

The toe of his boot made a line and brought to mind the notes he'd seen on Ophelia's desk when he'd visited her. Notes about runic magic.

Wait. He straightened and Ragewing, noticing his change in mood, uncovered him.

"I can draw it in the dirt!" Marius hurried over to Tahlia and Fara, hope making everything seem brighter.

He stole a stick from the fire, not caring that the end was red hot and smoking. Crouching, he began to write in the mud.

"Marius? What are you doing?" Tahlia leaned forward, her jasmine scent filling his nose and alerting his body to her nearness.

He scooted back and kept on writing.

Ophelia cursed me with illegal ancient magic. If I touch you, you will die. I don't recall why I came here, but now it feels as though the answer to breaking the curse lies in this terrible land. The curse won't allow me to speak of any of this.

Well, that was what he tried to write. But instead of those words, his scrawling only produced unreadable combinations of letters and symbols.

Standing, he shouted in rage and tossed the smoking and muddied stick into the darkness beyond the fire. Facing away from the others, he shuddered and swallowed against his tight throat. The rolling hills and fog-laced land stretched into the night, seemingly endless and dangerously barren. Ragewing let out a grumble and the ground trembled slightly under what must have been a stomp.

"You promise to leave tomorrow, yes?" He couldn't turn back around to look at Tahlia. It was too much. He felt as though Ophelia had snapped his ribs, reached into his chest, and removed half his heart. The other half belonged to Ragewing and it beat sluggishly, dying a slow death on its own.

"Maybe."

"Ah, right. You can lie." He hadn't intended for his words to hold the ire they did, but he was just so damned irritated with this curse.

"Easy now, HC. Don't treat me like Maiwenn does. I'm not lying to you."

"You said you would leave after one day. You already lied."

"I didn't say after which day."

Fara snorted. "Now, that is the Fae side of you talking there."

Marius ran his hands through his tangled hair and whirled to face the females and the dragons. "I'm sorry I'm behaving like a madman."

"Not a madman," Tahlia said as she stoked the fire, "just like someone with a big problem who takes it out on everyone around them."

A pang of regret hit Marius's already severely injured heart. "I said I'm sorry."

"Show it." Tahlia met his gaze, her eyes burning.

"HC?" Fara whispered.

"High Captain," Tahlia whispered back.

"Oh, right," Fara said.

Tahlia stood, and though she didn't come closer, she felt closer to Marius somehow. "You said you care deeply for me, yes?"

Fara's eyes widened, then she rose quickly and went to the dragons, muttering about poultices.

"I did. I do," Marius said, the curse creeping up his throat again to snare his tongue. His feelings for Tahlia were tied to this dark magic. Of that, he had no doubt.

Tahlia's eyes shuttered briefly as if his words were a balm. He took a slow breath. He should have been saying that and more to her every moment they were together, back when he still could speak freely. He'd thought they had all the time in the world.

"So," Tahlia continued, "how do you expect me to leave you here like this? I feel for you as much as you feel for me. Possibly a great deal more."

"Not possible."

Her lovely dusky-rose-hued lips formed a sad smile.

"I can't watch you die for me," he said.

"I'm a Mist Knight. You probably will watch me die at some point."

"That's for the order. For the realm. I won't have your life shortened because... I can't..." Shaking and baring his teeth, he fisted his hands until his knuckles nearly broke the skin.

Tahlia lifted a hand. "Eh, breathe. I know what you mean. Because of whatever is going on with you specifically."

"So you agree to leave tomorrow?"

"Not at all."

He threw up his hands and paced a circle. "Of course."

"I understand what you're saying, but I don't agree with it. If I were in your place, would you stay for me? Would you and Ragewing risk all for me?"

He halted. "You know I would."

"I didn't realize that."

"Well," he said, tongue burning as his desire to tell her about the curse and the cause rose again, "you do now."

"Don't expect any less of me than you do of yourself. Don't degrade me like that."

"I, Tahlia, I..."

"You were trying to tell me about whatever is happening by drawing in the mud, weren't you?"

"Yes." Pain shot down his throat.

"We will figure this out. Now, why don't you sleep and I'll take the first watch. Fara, will you take second?"

"Aye."

Tahlia nodded, looking like she was the highest rank here and enjoying the feeling of leadership. A reluctant grin tugged at one side of his mouth.

"I won't sleep, but I'll try." Marius hated this, but he couldn't argue. He would do the same if he was in her boots. "But first, I need to wash."

Her gaze tingled between his shoulder blades as he walked down the sloping, mossy ground toward the small creek. He had heard that once you choose your mate, you become incredibly sensitive to their presence. Shaking his head, he hoped he hadn't doomed her. She should be with someone who wasn't wrapped in a madwoman's snare. Someone kind who laughed more than he did. She deserved joy. Not this mess. But jealous pangs hit him as he imagined such a pairing. No matter what, he wanted her for himself. Even while he hated himself for the emotion.

After washing his dirt-smeared hands and face, he did his best to wash the mud from his trousers. When he returned to their camp, he settled himself across the fire from Fara, and Tahlia took up a spot on the nearest log. She gave him a sweet smile as he stretched out on the sturdy old bedroll he always brought on missions.

"This roll smells like the disgusting sausages Titus loves," Marius said.

Tahlia and Fara chuckled.

"Can't wait to try one," Tahlia said. "Do you think we will be called to attack soon?"

He knew she was attempting to help him imagine a future when they were past this experience.

"I do. Very soon." Likely, they'd miss the first call. What would the other riders do when they realized Marius, Tahlia, and Fara were missing?

Gods, he hoped he'd see his friend Titus again and with his own mind intact and Tahlia on his arm. He drifted into musings, his thoughts floating away like sparks in the wind.

CHAPTER 16
TAHLIA

Tahlia bolted upright on her bedroll and whipped her head toward where Marius had been sitting when she'd finally given up and fallen asleep. He was still there. Phew. She hated the idea of sleeping while he was up, but she and Fara had both been far too tired to stay awake.

"How are you feeling?" she asked Marius over Fara's snoring.

The dawn was just over the horizon and the sky had begun to lighten.

Marius looked at the last dregs of the fire, the smoke rising around him like he'd been on fire too. "I'm fine."

"Sure."

He had the look of a man who'd been hit on the back of the head by something very heavy. Like someone who had memory issues from an injury.

"I am," he insisted.

"No missing pieces from your watch? No lapses in memory?"

"Not that I can recall."

He was hiding something. It was obvious in the way he wouldn't look directly at her. "What's bothering you, then? I mean, besides whatever is going on with your ability to tell me things and this whole dark adventure."

"My hands are dirty."

"Who cares? We are miles from anyone who might change their opinion of your tidy arse."

"I washed them before sleeping. Now look at them." He splayed his fingers and she walked closer to look.

Dirt lined the spaces between his large fingers and his nails held a line of mud too.

"Hmm. Well, it is muddy here. Maybe you just picked something up? Like your bedroll?" He had already packed it away apparently. "Perhaps you didn't notice when it was full dark. Or you tried to write more in the mud when you were out of it? Anyway, I'm awake now, so if you want to return to the creek to wash up, it's certainly fine with me."

He turned and grabbed a parcel wrapped in waxed linen. "Eat this. You and Fara. I already had my share."

When he lobbed the package, Tahlia caught it neatly and opened it up. A square of honeyed bread dotted with pieces of fig sat inside. Tahlia's stomach growled.

Marius walked away, Ragewing trailing him.

"What is that?" Fara was suddenly sitting up and wide awake.

"Oh, just a little treat Marius has offered us." Tahlia handed a corner of the bread over.

Fara gobbled it down, groaning in ecstasy. Tahlia

laughed and they worked their way through half the square.

"I'm going to give the rest to Vodolija."

Fara grumbled but nodded and began to tie up her bedroll.

Fog crept across the dark green and gray landscape, the tops of the distant trees poking up through the misty white like fingers from a shallow grave. A chill wrapped around Tahlia, but it didn't alarm her. This place was haunted and she would have been more worried if she hadn't felt the chill. At this point, fear and fretting were the norm.

Vodolija stood over a cluster of large and mossy stones. She eyed a ferret-like creature that was darting between the rocks and nibbling greenery.

"How does that wee thing not even notice the massive predator staring down at him hungrily?"

The Seabreak grunted, a dragon's version of a shrug. Then she moved, her head lashing out like a great arrow, and the ferret was gone.

"Ew." Tahlia turned away to let the dragon finish her breakfast. "I was going to offer you a bit of honey and fig bread, but you seem to be just fine."

The dragon bumped her back and she spun to see expectant eyes.

"Fine. I suppose it can be your dessert." Tahlia opened her palm and Vodolija nibbled the bread with the tip of her smooth, scaly snout.

"She's going to take a finger someday," Fara said from behind.

"I don't know. I haven't seen any riders missing

fingers. Oh, wait, I do think there was someone who was missing a thumb."

"Exactly. With you being part human, you'll probably be the next victim."

"Gee, thank you for that."

"Just warning you. Not saying I want it to happen. I'm not Ophelia."

"She doesn't just want my finger. She wants my life."

"Fair. Then maybe I should have said I'm not Maiwenn."

"Accurate."

Fara laughed sadly and offered Tahlia a steaming cup of what smelled like pine needle tea. They drank in silence as the fog circled Vodolija and their view of the slope that led to the creek.

"He's been gone a while," Fara said.

"Not really. Let's pack up and be ready to move on when he returns." Tahlia said, leading Fara back to the fire.

"What is the plan exactly?" Fara finished her tea, shook the cup, and tucked it into the middling-sized satchel they'd brought along with the smaller ones they could affix to themselves if needed. They also had a larger bag tied onto Vodolija.

"I am really not sure," Tahlia said. "I guess we'll try to get Marius to return."

"And if he refuses?"

"We'll follow him wherever he feels led to go."

"So we are putting the madman in charge of the quest."

"Only way to see what's happening."

"You sound so nonchalant considering you're wandering a dead kingdom full of ghosts."

"Don't forget. You chose to come with me."

Fara bunched her lips and whispered something that was most likely a gentle curse aimed in Tahlia's direction.

Marius returned and Tahlia didn't want to admit how relieved she was to see him. Was he really fine now?

"How was the creek?"

"I spotted a ruined fortress. We should explore it."

"Why?" Fara asked. She closed her fist over her mouth. "I meant, what do you expect to find, High Captain?"

"I'm not certain, but I feel led to visit it, so if you refuse to leave, you might as well come as backup." Marius gathered his things and they tied their bags to the dragons.

"How does it feel?" Tahlia asked, eyeing him. He seemed distracted and nothing about that put her at ease.

"The pull?"

"Yes."

"Like extreme curiosity."

The craving to go to him, to hold him, to feel the heat of his body against hers, hit Tahlia like a punch to the heart. She took a shuddering breath and he looked up from checking Ragewing's girth buckle.

"Or you can remain here?" he asked softly.

Fara had moved to the other side of Vodolija to apply some poultice where the saddle rubbed. She'd already done so on this side.

His scent wafted through the air. She fought the urge to go to him and the desire to let go of worrying about whatever was going on with him. She forced her feet to remain where they were.

"No, we are going with you."

He nodded and climbed onto Ragewing's back, his movements quick and easy. Fara came back around Vodolija and they mounted the Seabreak and readied to take off.

The dragons soared out of the fog and into the dull light of the morning sky.

CHAPTER 17
MARIUS

The tug on Marius's soul felt like so much more than curiosity, but he hadn't wanted to further alarm Tahlia and Fara. This sensation was not a tickle of interest but more like a dragon had sunk his talons into Marius's very being and dragged him to the timeworn fortress below.

To calm his own fast pulse, Marius set a hand on Ragewing's warm scales. Ragewing raised his head and grunted. He extended a wing and held off a blast of cool wind and mist, protecting Marius in a way that had him swallowing against a lump in his throat. He was so grateful for Ragewing, for Tahlia, and even for Fara and her dire warnings and inexperience. He didn't think he deserved their loyalty, but he was incredibly glad for it.

They landed amid the fog that didn't seem to be ready to lift anytime soon. Tahlia dismounted and helped Fara down.

Four stone towers stood in a rough square. The weather-eaten remains of what had once been wooden walls stretched to each one. A variety of circular stone buildings dotted the area. One appeared to be a dovecote, another a kitchen with the domed stove still intact, and a taller one in the back had possibly been a chapel. The wind whistled through a plow someone had pulled into the old fortress and a bronze chain clanked against one of the towers. A thousand mysteries could be hiding in these ruins. Trunks of gold and jewels might be just beneath their feet.

"Ooooh, spooky. I like it."

Fara threw up her hands. "Of course you think this haunted nightmare is great. You probably want to settle in and roast marshmallows." Her wide stare slid over the wind-blown weeds growing by a forgotten well.

It was a wishing well, complete with a wooden arch decorated with constellations. Tahlia wandered over.

Marius's view of the females blurred like his vision had been marred by drink, so he squeezed his eyes shut, trying to clear the fuzziness away. He opened his eyes again and blinked. His vision was better, but not yet normal.

"Marius?" Tahlia came closer, but thankfully, not too close.

He held out a hand. "Just give me a minute."

But instead of taking a breath and gathering himself, his feet moved of their own accord. He stalked toward the well.

"Marius?" Tahlia shouted and ran up beside him.

Fara, still near Vodolija, was saying something, but the whispers of strange voices echoed in his ears. The hairs on the back of his neck rose.

"Stay back," he said, barely able to hear his own voice.

He looked down into the black of the old well, and a sense of evil slithered over his skin. Ragewing came up beside him, growling, nostrils loosing tendrils of smoke. The dragon spit sparks into the well. The bits of fire danced down and disappeared. The whispers rose, louder and louder and louder. With voices like rocks cracking against each other, they spoke in a language Marius didn't know. The sensation of evil's presence increased. A weight on his chest, on his shoulders, the foul and invisible essence turned his stomach and brought on a cold sweat that slicked his face.

Shadows burst from the well and blew Marius, Tahlia, Fara, and the dragons backward.

"Not a wishing well! Not a wishing welllll!" Tahlia shouted, scrambling to unsheathe her sword.

Somehow the wispy essence pouring from the well had a heaviness to it. The sentient, ragged cloud of evil zipped past Marius, then down again to release a gust of wind. Marius stumbled and nearly fell. Tahlia grabbed Fara to keep her upright. The shadows whirled around the air above Vodolija's head, then dipped and shot at Fara.

Heart pounding and ears ringing with the voices, Marius lunged and put himself between the shadows and Fara. Tahlia shouted something Marius couldn't hear.

Everything slowed. The shadows were going to unmake him. He knew it. They were pure evil. He drew his sword though it was likely worthless.

The shadows split and flowed around Marius like a river of night. His hands sparked with what felt like fire. He dropped his sword. Golden light crackled from his fingertips as he spun, and the shadows gathered overhead. With no idea what was happening, he lifted his hands. The golden light snapped upward and shattered the shadows into a thousand pieces. The wind pulled the bulk of the evil apart and the voices at last fell into silence.

"What in all the realms was that?" Tahlia was panting and holding Fara's arm.

"We should leave now before whatever it was returns." Fara drew away from Tahlia and started toward Vodolija.

Marius's arms ached to pull Tahlia to him and to make certain she was well and whole. "Are you all right?"

Tahlia nodded. "What just happened with your hands?"

"I assume it's... The..." The heat of frustration swallowed him and he swore creatively.

Fara waved from her spot beside the Seabreak. "I don't know about sons of bastard mountain goats, but I like the sentiment. Let's fly."

"We can't leave," Tahlia said. "We have to figure out what that was and how it's tied to Marius."

Marius wanted to chime in and agree, to add his thoughts, but his tongue refused, the contents of his mind straying to the curse and its unseen rules. He bowed his head and tried to breathe through his impotent anger. Ragewing came close and extended a wing over him. He set a hand on the dragon's scales and comfort flowed into him, easing his tension.

"The shadows struck out at you and Fara," Tahlia said. "That's what you saw too?"

Marius grunted to confirm.

"But they ignored me and they didn't harm you when you defended Fara. It was like you were untouchable. They didn't even seem to notice me."

"Why are you calling a cloud of shadows *they*?" Fara asked.

"I'm not sure," Tahlia said. "I sense that it was a collection of beings. Do you agree, Marius?"

He nodded, not trusting his tongue. But maybe he could tell her a few things. He had to try. "I heard voices. Did you?"

"No." Tahlia frowned and studied his face, her smooth brow wrinkling as she pondered. He loved how she looked when she was thinking.

Fara shuddered. "Please. Let's get into the sky and away from this place."

Tahlia waved an impatient hand at Fara. "This is exciting. I'm not going back to sit by a fire and wait until whatever comes at us. I'd rather meet it head-on."

Groaning, Fara returned to Tahlia's side.

"It was another language," Marius managed to say despite the tightening in his throat and the strangling feel of the dark magic on him.

A slender shadow rose from the well and slithered toward them.

"Another one!" Fara shouted.

Marius was already lifting his hands. The golden

light once again flashed from his fingers and palms, chasing the last shadow. But the shadow didn't dissipate. It just hovered over them, not attacking, but not breaking into pieces like the others had.

"Is it coming for me?" Fara had shut her eyes, but she was holding up her fists like she was ready for a boxing match.

"I don't think so," Tahlia said, studying the slip of darkness.

Marius growled at the shadow. It seemed to shiver, growing more transparent. Then it zipped away.

The evil sensation that had Marius in its grip increased in intensity. It wrapped him in a shroud of confusion and the world blurred. An invisible chain latched onto his heart and pulled hard.

CHAPTER 18
TAHLIA

A humming, howling sound similar to the one they'd heard earlier started up, coming from the forest and sending shivers down Tahlia's spine.

A flash of light forced her eyes shut.

She opened them as quickly as she could.

Fara was gone.

And so were Marius and Ragewing.

Panic lanced Tahlia and she held her breath. "Where did they go, Vodolija?"

The Seabreak tossed her head, sniffed the air, then eyed the sky. Ragewing and Marius were far above. They must have taken off in a bout of mind-boggling speed. Already, they were a blur flying over the fog. How had he mounted up that quickly? And where was Fara? Had time passed somehow while Tahlia's eyes were closed against the light?

Ice flowed through her stomach.

"Fara!"

She ran through the fortress, eyes not moving fast enough and her lungs tightening with fear.

Kicking down the door of the first tower she came to, she called out, "Fara! Please answer me!"

But there was only a broken stool, moldy crates cloaked in dust, and the musty air of a land long devoid of life. As she searched the other three towers, she replayed the last moments in her head. The humming. The light. Had the light been related to the illumination that had shot from Marius's hands when the shadows attacked? She didn't know. It had been bright, but she hadn't had time to see the hue of the illumination.

Back in the open area, she lifted a hand to Vodolija. "Did you see anything?"

Vodolija grunted at the ground. But there was nothing there.

"What is it?"

Tahlia circled the area, but not even a footprint marred the muddy spot. Only dirt and a scraggly plant with thick blood-red leaves. Vodolija bumped her from behind, urging her closer to the spot.

"I'm so confused. We don't have time for this. We might be able to spot Fara. We'll search for Ragewing and Marius afterward since a dragon is easier to spot than one skinny Fae female."

Vodolija tossed her head and sparked fire.

"Don't be angry with me. I don't understand."

The dragon lowered a wing and shoulder, allowing Tahlia to climb up into the saddle, but she was obviously perturbed. She blew a spout of flame, bright in the dark.

"Please. We can figure out whatever you're trying to

tell me later. Let's get up high and see if we can spot Fara. She can't have gone far." Or been taken far.

A shiver grabbed hold of Tahlia and shook her hard. Had the ghosts of this wild place taken her? And if so, what would they do to her?

Vodolija took off and Tahlia studied the land beneath them. She tapped the dragon's neck, indicating she should fly over the forest. It was too dark to see anything really, but what else could she do? It wasn't as if she could just leave Fara. Her palms grew damp and she fidgeted with the reins. The air was wet and cold and that first shiver of fear had turned into a constant, uncomfortable trembling. Trees, trees, and more trees. There was no sign of Fara anywhere.

"Fly toward Ragewing!" she called out to Vodolija. "We'll get him and then come back for Fara."

Why had Marius taken off without warning? Had he seen Fara stolen by something? Or was he leaving for a different reason entirely? Gods, Tahlia had more questions than could be answered in one dark night. Panic seared her nerves and made her lower herself on Vodolija's neck. She longed for comfort, for heat, for the ability to turn back time and keep Marius from leaving in the first place. She should have fought with him, demanded answers. Anything to keep him from whatever this was. Then Fara would have been safe at the keep too instead of only the gods knew where.

Tahlia silently prayed for her friend as Ragewing and Marius came into view.

The wind whipped Tahlia's cloak around despite its many clasps and she fought to keep her teeth from cracking as they chattered violently from both worry and cold. Vodolija flew into a bank of ragged clouds and Tahlia lost sight of Marius and Ragewing.

"Damned clouds!"

She squinted and stood in the stirrups, trying in vain to see more than mist and inconsistent light. If she lost them, what was she going to do? Vodolija's body rumbled with a trilling purr and Tahlia resumed her seat.

Tahlia was aware her mind wasn't operating at a top notch level. Panic pinched at her confidence. "I'm trying to be calm. It's not easy."

The Seabreak snorted and blew a cloud of smoke. Tahlia set a hand on her warm scales and kept her eyes peeled for any sign of them. A scream of fear and frustration built inside her chest, but she bit it back, gulping down her worry and trying to remember that she was a Mist Knight. She could handle this.

When they broke through the cover, Tahlia spotted Marius and Ragewing.

She exhaled and finally stopped gripping the reins with her right hand. She cracked her knuckles and spoke to Vodolija.

"They're landing. Do you see them?"

The glowing light flickered, the odd shine emanating from a caldera. From where did the glow originate? Random spots on the ground?

Vodolija soared down toward the rocky formation and landed a few feet from Ragewing. Marius had leapt from his dragon's back and was tearing at the muddy earth with his hands. Tahlia dismounted, keeping an eye on their surroundings. The air vibrated with something unnameable—magic? Or something under the ground? No, it was more than a physical disturbance in the area. This barren spot felt raw and wrong. The golden light flickered over Marius's hands, reminding Tahlia of... Of what?

Then Marius shouted, his words unintelligible. Ragewing roared and stomped his feet as if agitated. Rightly so. Vodolija nuzzled against Ragewing, then swung toward Tahlia and pushed her with the edge of a wing. That red-leafed plant grew here too.

"What is it with you and this plant?"

She strode away, hurrying to Marius's side even though she wasn't sure this was the right move. What was he digging for?

The golden light created a shimmering border along oddly shaped stones set into the dirt. No, this wasn't a rock formation.

They were bones.

But not just regular bones. The one Marius was attempting to dislodge was a femur, but it was longer than a dragon's. Much, much longer. A gnarled skull sat halfway out of the ground and a twisted spine looked like it was about to crawl out of the mud. Ah, and there were hands. Very large hands.

Tahlia shivered violently.

These had to be the bones of a giant.

Giants had existed outside of old children's stories? Well, here was evidence that they certainly had. Were these bones related to why the Kingdom of Spirits had become the nightmare that it was? Had a huge monster ravaged these lands? But the bigger question was why Marius was attempting to dig up the giant's bones…

Wait. He had been wondering about his dirty hands when they'd camped. Had he already been here?

Swallowing her fear, she started to put a hand on Marius's shoulder. He swung around and fell back. His eyes were wide, and his temples glittered with the same golden light that flickered across his hands and along the half-buried bones.

Tahlia stood frozen, the bitter taste of fear on the back of her tongue.

"Don't," he growled, his voice low and his eyes vacant and glimmering with gold light. "Lady Tahlia…" He didn't blink. It was like he wasn't himself at all.

"Marius, what are you doing?" The urge to shake him was nearly overpowering, but he obviously didn't want her to touch him, so she held the hilt of her gladius instead.

He bent his head, shook it, then stood. When he raised his chin and his eyes met hers, the golden light was gone from his head and hands. The odd illumination continued to glimmer around the bones.

"I, I don't know." He looked like a wild animal about to attack.

"Ragewing, please pick up your rider," Tahlia said, still facing Marius in case he lost his mind and did something crazy.

CHAPTER 19
TAHLIA

Ragewing didn't hesitate. He lifted into the air, then snatched up Marius in his front talons and began flying out of the caldera. They disappeared behind the rocky walls of the bowl-shaped area.

Heart thumping like mad, Tahlia ran to Vodolija. The dragon eased back, lowered her head, and snorted at the red-leafed plant again.

"Fine!" Tahlia plucked a bunch of it and held it high. "Are you happy now?"

The Seabreak moved her jaws.

"What does that mean? We are going to lose Marius and Ragewing. We don't have time to chitchat, darling. What is that motion? Eating?" She eyed the plant that was half crushed in her hand. Did Vodolija want her to eat it? "Why? What is this plant?"

The dragon nudged her belly, then blew smoke over her face.

"Fine. Whatever. If I die, I'm going to haunt your tail for eternity." She bit off a small piece of leaf. Cinnamon and anise danced over her tongue, which wasn't too horrible really, but it was dry and difficult to swallow. She finally managed it. A tingling spread across her forehead and down the back of her head. She cleared her throat, tongue stinging slightly.

She held out her hands to Vodolija. "Happy now?"

I am, actually.

Tahlia fell back a step. Had she just...

Yes, that's me. Vodolija. Your bonded dragon and the one who loves you best of all.

The Seabreak trilled and lowered her shoulder and wing.

"What in all the realms? How did this happen? Am I losing my mind like Marius seems to be?" Tahlia eyed the plant again. "How? Why?"

We should probably take off sometime this year, Tahlia.

That was her dragon. Talking to her inside her mind. She couldn't seem to move.

Snap out of it, rider! Get on my back and let's get to the males.

Stuttering nonsense, Tahlia did as Vodolija suggested and soon they were airborne. "You love me?"

Of course I do. I wouldn't risk my life for you on this mad quest if I didn't.

Tahlia's heart warmed. This was incredible! She rubbed the smooth deep blue stripe of scales beside the saddle. "Do you know anything about what happened to Fara or where she might be? And what do you think is wrong with Marius and why is Ragewing putting up with it?"

I don't have any more information about Fara than you

do. Although, if you recall, she is the one who told you about this plant that allows us to speak to one another. Remember?

Oh. Yes. She had mentioned blood-red leaves and something about bonding with dragons. Tahlia could strangle herself for not listening better to her friend.

I have to find her, Vodolija. Tahlia's blood felt like the icy water of the high mountains.

She was there and then she was gone, Vodolija said. *There was a delicate presence around us when she disappeared though. Perhaps a ghost? As for Marius, he has a foul energy to him. He needs time with the clear crystals.*

They cleared the caldera. Marius and Ragewing were not too far off.

"I thought the crystals only help dragons."

I think you know very well that they also affect Fae. Even half-Fae.

Tahlia's cheeks flushed. "How did you know about that?"

I have been slightly linked with you since the first day I chose you.

"Really? Is that how all dragons and riders work?"

You're thinking of the new commander and her dragon.

"I am."

He will not bond with her fully, but they are linked tentatively. He thought she would grow wiser, but she has only become more evil.

"I believe she killed her father."

You're probably right, but the dragons don't know. Well, her dragon won't communicate with the rest of us. He hasn't since you joined the order.

Tahlia poised herself to remain balanced in the

saddle as Vodolija soared toward the ground, aiming for Ragewing and Marius's landing spot beside a small river. He had dismounted and started walking toward the water.

"I have so many questions, but they will likely need to wait. But, umm, can I call you Lija for short?"

Yes. I quite like that.

"Do you know Ophelia's dragon's name?"

I do.

"But you can't tell me."

I will not. It is against our ways.

"I understand."

You spoke to me through your mind a moment ago. Did you notice? Lija said.

"No. I did?"

Yes. Try again.

Can you hear me?

I can. Speaking like this might tire you at first. But you will grow used to it.

Thank you. For being patient with me.

Of course. You are my chosen rider.

Warmth battled with the cold fear in Tahlia's chest.

Lija alighted on the mossy ground and Tahlia hurried to climb off. She went to where Marius stood looking into the water.

"Marius? Are you all right?"

He was staring at the reflection of his face. "I can't..." His lips pulled back and he lifted his head, growling in frustration.

He is cursed. You know that, yes? Lija said.

Cursed? "I know he is hurting somehow and that

something was wrong. What type of curse? Who cursed him and why? What can I do to help? Why won't he talk to me about it? Is he unable?"

Slow down, rider.

"Sorry."

"Who are you talking to?" Marius asked. He continued staring at the water and his rippling visage. "I... I don't know... Where..." He looked up, his eyes going hazy and gold again.

Ragewing says Marius knows Ophelia cursed him. Marius felt called to travel here.

Called? Tahlia asked Lija.

That is how it feels to Ragewing. As if some power has reached out to the High Captain and is luring him to this foul, barren land.

"Marius, we have to find Fara. Something took her or... I don't know. But she's gone and she isn't exactly an adventurer. If you can handle setting whatever you're dealing with aside for a bit, we should go look for her. Can you do that? Can you promise me you won't go back to that caldera and mess with those scary as hells bones again?"

"I don't know. I can't, I cannot seem to really... I can't talk."

"I know. Vodolija told me." He needed the same ability with Ragewing. It might make it possible for him to speak to Ragewing about the problem, at least. Tahlia searched the ground for that blood-red plant and came up empty. "I have a solution to some of this, but I can't take the time for that at the moment. I have to find Fara."

"Agreed." Marius's face was back to its stormy self

and, gods, but she was happy to see it. "But then you must leave. You'll go once we find her."

"Of course," Tahlia lied.

They mounted and began to fly back toward the place where Fara had disappeared.

As they traveled, the dragons staying low, their bellies nearly scraping the clusters of scrubby trees here and there, the sound started again—a quiet howling and humming that grew in volume.

CHAPTER 20
TAHLIA

A golden light flickered below them, beside what looked like the ruins of an old castle. Marius looked to Tahlia and motioned to the light. She nodded and their dragons began to dive. Ragewing came to a stop on what had once been a rutted cart path. The two lines of expertly laid rock were now mostly covered with the greenish-black moss that seemed to grow everywhere here. Lija perched on a tumble of rounded building stones. Both riders remained on their mounts as the strange light approached. The illumination morphed into an outline of a Fae male.

The ethereal Fae had large ram horns that curled away from his pleasant-looking face. He had cheekbones like Fara's, sharp but not long. His hair and his skin were fashioned of that same golden light, as was his cloak and the simple leather boots that stuck out at the bottom of the woolen wrap. A thick torc shimmered around his neck, a traditional accessory that the Fae of the king's city still wore today.

"A ghost?" Tahlia suggested out loud to Lija. Speaking through minds was difficult. She'd had to get used to it.

Marius glanced her way, a mix of sadness, hope, and wonder crossing his features and clouding his eyes. He looked like he wanted to grab her and leave here without helping anyone do anything. Her heart surged, pushing her from her saddle and off Lija's back. But he, like Tahlia, had to know that wasn't possible.

"I think so," he said.

Tahlia found her footing off the pile of stones. Marius must have thought she was talking to him, of course, because he didn't know about the plant and all of that madness.

The ghost is quite old, Lija said into Tahlia's mind, *but his spirit is bright and full of life.*

"Vodolija says he is bright, which I'd guess means he's not a kidnapper of friends." *Fara, please be all right,* she prayed silently.

Marius dismounted and paused, hands still holding the reins. "Your dragon says?"

"Yes. That's a story for another time." Tahlia pointed at the spirit.

"Right." Marius cleared his throat and gave the ghost a shallow bow. "Spirit, we are searching for our friend, a female named Fara."

"She has purple skin, and dark hair, and is afraid of life in general. Have you seen her? Please say you have. She can't handle things like this."

Marius lifted an eyebrow at Tahlia.

The ghost floated farther away, his body partially obscured by the age-blackened remains of a gatehouse and wall. Vines grew over the stones and hung across the entrance like a curtain. The dragons flew over the old castle wall while Marius and Tahlia walked under the portcullis.

"That is why I have come to you," the spirit said. "Your friend is trapped below with the varjuline. They haven't drained her blood yet, but a portion of her spirit has been siphoned. Their feeding is accomplished through a dark, wordless magic. They glean blood and spirit from their victims and the wisps of energy and blood crawl through the very air and soak into the varjuline. They also save a portion of their victims' blood in bowls for Katk." The ghost pressed his eyes shut as if he'd seen the act and wished he hadn't.

Fear cut Tahlia again and again. "What are the varjuline?" Her voice had gone shrill. "Is that what those shadows are? We dealt with them once already. Is my friend alive?"

The ghost studied Tahlia, then Marius. "Oh, a whip. Fascinating." He raised a glowing eyebrow at Marius's favored weapon and grinned naughtily.

Tahlia waved both hands, impatient. "Please, focus. Tell us what to do."

The ghost rolled its eyes. Vodolija snorted and took a step toward the ghost.

"Easy, big beauty," the ghost said. Then he turned back to Tahlia. "Your friend still has a chance to live because she remembers her life and her center."

Tahlia exhaled, nearly falling to her knees in gratitude. Alive. Fara was alive and they were going to save her.

"That's what keeps me from becoming a varjuline," the ghost said, "which is a shadowling that exists only to feed themselves and to feed Katk. In life, I was called Trevain. Not that you asked."

A breeze that smelled like stagnant water drifted across Tahlia's face.

"Are they ghosts like you, but evil instead of oddly informative?" she asked, her hands shaking.

The ghost nodded, his partially transparent ram horns fading in and out. "As long as I retain my mind and my memories, I can withstand the call of the sleeping Katk."

"Enough talking," Marius said, drawing his sword. Ragewing flapped his wings, turning the area into a small windstorm for a moment. "We must rescue our squire."

Tahlia gave him a look, then smiled at the ghost. They wouldn't get far if they insulted anyone trying to help them. "We want to learn all about you, Trevain, but for now, can you take us to our friend?"

"I will do it for you," he said to Tahlia.

He bowed to her, then floated over a scattered floor of flagstones, moss, and earth.

An open doorway led to the remains of a staircase that descended underground. They trailed the spirit, the ghost's light illuminating the timeworn stone and the water dripping from the partially collapsed ceiling of the staircase. A corridor, as black as night, stretched out past the stairs. Marius remained in front of Tahlia, just behind Trevain.

"Stay back three steps," Marius ordered Tahlia over his shoulder.

"Aye, High Captain." She had to figure out why he was so insistent on not touching her.

The corridor opened into a chamber that smelled strongly of illness and blood.

Fara lay in the center of the room, surrounded by a cage of golden fire. They hurried inside, stopping at the ring.

"Fara?" Tahlia touched the ring. The flame didn't singe her skin, but the strange magic blocked her like a wall of stone.

Fara opened her eyes. "Tahlia?" She struggled to her feet and stared out at them through the flickering light. Her arms were covered in golden boils and instead of being the color of a rare amethyst, her skin was as pale as a shade-loving periwinkle bloom.

"You have only moments before the varjuline return," Trevain said, turning toward the doorway like he expected the villainous ghosts to enter this very second. "Though they will be less drawn to you, Tahlia, because of your human blood, there are many and they are hungry."

Tahlia unsheathed her short sword. "Move as far away from this edge as you can, Fara."

Fara did so and Tahlia swung her sword, aiming to slice through the flames. The sword passed through and Fara gasped, hope lighting her eyes. But the flames returned before she could escape.

"Damn it!" Tahlia whirled. "Marius, any ideas?"

"High Captain. Please."

"Really? You're worried about rules and regulations at a time like this?"

"This is exactly the time to remain disciplined and to follow protocol. That's all we have to rely on when so much is out of our control."

"All you might have to rely on, but rules don't always work toward an end goal." Exasperated, she waved her hands. "Just forget about that. What do we do?"

Marius stepped closer to Fara. "What happened? Who trapped you here?"

"I told you. It was the varjuline," Trevain said.

"Apologies, but I don't trust you yet," Marius snapped over his shoulder.

Tahlia gave Marius a look. "Sorry, Trevain," she said, glancing the ghost's way. "He's a bit of a grouch. He does trust you, or he wouldn't have followed you in here. He especially wouldn't have let me trail along. He's very protective."

Trevain nodded. "I know that type. The whip also says a lot."

Marius's eyes were lightning. "Will you please remain on task?"

Tahlia studied Fara, her chest caving at the color of her skin. "Fara, we will get you out of here."

Fara coughed and a spot of blood showed on her bottom lip. "Dark shadows..." More coughing interrupted her and she crumbled to the chamber's stone floor.

"Fara," Marius said, his voice stern but somehow

incredibly comforting, "Lady Tahlia speaks the truth. We will free you. Have no doubt."

Tahlia melted inside. If only they could be back at the keep, feasting or flying or both. She hated seeing her two favorite people in such agony.

Fara only nodded, seemingly unable to say anything else.

"Duck your head down," Marius ordered her. He faced Tahlia. "Take my sword. It will strike a wider path. Once you cut the flames, I will lunge for her."

"You can touch her?" Tahlia asked.

Marius's eyes shuttered for a second like her words had struck him a mortal blow.

"He is only cursed to never touch you," Trevain said.

Tahlia whirled. "What do you mean? You know what's wrong with him?"

"It's insulting that your knee-jerk reaction is to think I'm an idiot just because I'm not quite alive."

"That's not," Tahlia started to say, "that's not what I meant, I—"

The ghost waved her apology away. "I know some things. For instance, Katk is trying to rise. A new champion has awakened him from his long slumber, as evidenced by the activity of the varjuline."

"I'm so confused," Tahlia said. "Let's put a pin in that for now. How can we get Fara out?"

"You'll need a really big pin for that one..." Trevain exhaled, clearly annoyed. "I have never witnessed anyone escaping a varjuline's cage."

Tahlia's heart sank.

"Then ready yourself, Lady Tahlia." Marius set his sword on the ground.

She picked it up. The hilt was still warm from his hand. She bit her lip, praying and wishing and begging all of the Old Ones to come to their aid with this whole mess.

Tahlia swung Marius's longer, wider sword along the middle of the cage. The flames sputtered and cut out and Marius moved in a blur of astounding speed, his arms reaching down for Fara. He grunted in pain and drew back just as quickly as the flames reignited themselves.

"I can't do it. They're too quick to reform."

"If they're too fast for you, they're too quick for anything in any realm. You are so incredibly fast, Marius. I mean, High Captain."

Marius's stone face gave none of his thoughts away.

"Do the creatures fear any force or being?" he asked Trevain, even though his gaze was on Tahlia. She felt his look like a hand on her cheek, and to steady herself, she took a deep breath.

"Only their master, Katk."

Marius made a quiet humming noise like he was thinking. "What does he wield?"

"Plague, of course." Trevain gestured to Fara.

"Well, I don't have experience wielding illness," Tahlia said, "aside from sneezing on folks when I have an ague."

"It's a bit more serious than that, I'm afraid," Trevain said.

Oh, how Tahlia wanted to hear Fara say something

dark and worrisome. She looked awful, slumped inside the cage of flames.

"Maybe we should fight fire with fire?" Tahlia ran from the chamber, heading for the dragons.

Vodolija? Tahlia tried to speak to the Seabreak inside her head again. *Lija?* No answer. Perhaps Tahlia needed more practice.

"Vodolija?" she called out as soon as she was back in the remains of the great hall.

The dragon flew over the half-collapsed roof, then dove into the great hall, her wings barely able to work in the broken space.

Marius and Trevain ran up behind Tahlia.

She climbed onto Lija, scrambling to the saddle. "We need to get the chamber uncovered so they can try their fire on the cage."

"Worth a try," Marius said quickly.

Howling erupted outside the walls. Goosebumps ran the length of Tahlia's body.

Trevain grew even more transparent. "They're here. The varjuline. I don't know if they can hurt your dragons, but you, you must flee!"

Staring the ghost down, Tahlia shook her head. "I'm not leaving Fara."

"We don't abandon our own," Marius said.

Ragewing hovered above the ruins, wings blowing the spindly branches of a tree growing out of the wall.

"Which is why I haven't left you yet, High Captain," Tahlia said, climbing onto Lija's back.

Marius growled and showed his fangs to Tahlia, then he leapt onto Ragewing.

Black shadows coursed into the old keep, their movements like oil seeping into the empty spaces in the walls and spreading over the floor, only to crest like waves. When they peaked, their Fae-like silhouettes had heads, flowing hair in varying lengths, arms, and torsos.

"Gods, they are creepy. Lija, try frying them."

I like that plan.

The Seabreak's four wings fluttered as she flew out of the ruins and hovered beside Ragewing. Both dragons blew fire into the oily shadows, but the dark shapes fled before the fire could hit them.

"They are running from the flames, so it must hurt them," Tahlia called out to Marius. "Can you not use that power you wielded last time?"

"I will attempt it." He lifted his hands, but no sparkling magic flashed.

Damn. She guessed he couldn't control whatever that power was.

Shaking his head, he pulled his whip from his shoulder and let it whirl and crack over the area where the varjuline had gathered. They didn't dart away from the whip's end like they had from the fire, but their heads had turned.

Marius locked his gaze on Tahlia. "At the same time."

She knew what he meant. He'd crack the whip and distract them while the dragons breathed fire again.

Marius raised his arm, but a shadow shot from the group and curled around his hand. He shouted, obviously in pain.

Had the shadows learned from the first battle? Did they know that Marius, possibly because of his curse, could wield magic? Were they taking action against that power somehow?

He shook his hand, but the shadow clung tightly. His grimace told her that the shadow's touch poured agony into him. Ragewing flew higher, and finally, the varjuline dropped away from Marius. His whip hand looked paler. He put his whip in his other hand, then unleashed it with a crack.

The varjuline eyed the whip, their motions almost in sync.

"Now," Tahlia said to Lija.

Lija and Ragewing blew fire into the varjuline. They scattered, their forms ragged and bits of their essence floating into the air like clouds of ash.

"Again!" Marius commanded. He cracked the whip twice this time, once on his right and then on his left.

The varjuline howled and Tahlia's ears rang. Lija and Ragewing let loose two more streams of blazing fire, and the varjuline were no more.

"Quick, Lija, tear up the stones there. Open the place up!"

The Seabreak dove, smashed her talons into the old floor, and rose back into the air. Tahlia couldn't see beneath her mount, but Lija must have been holding a few good scoops of dislodged rock because some of the debris was missing. Fara slumped, lifeless, in the fiery cage below the broken floor.

Ragewing and Lija flew down to the next level, landing beside the cage.

Marius flexed the hand the varjuline had attacked. "On my count, flame."

"Stay down, Fara!" Tahlia hoped she would remain where she was. She didn't want their proposed solution to be worse than the problem.

"One, two, three!" Marius called out with Trevain now hovering just behind him and Ragewing.

The flames from both dragons mingled to create a river of fire colored citrine, sapphire, ruby, and aquamarine. Fara's head lolled to one side, then she ducked again, hands over her head protectively. The cage shimmered, grew brighter, then dissolved like the creatures who had built it.

Marius leapt from Ragewing, gathered Fara into his arms, then took off. Tahlia and Lija followed close behind with Trevain streaming along beside them.

At the first area of ground covered in moss and low grasses, they landed, Tahlia and Lija quickly getting a fire going for Fara and making her as comfortable as possible considering evil ghosts were lurking about and they only had one heavy blanket between all their bags.

Fara sat up against a boulder. Marius tucked the fine blanket around her. Silver embroidery sewn into cloud-like patterns decorated the top-notch wool. He stood and turned to face the ghost.

"Trevain, do you know a remedy for what ails her?"

A small shadow oozed from the ground and Marius leapt back.

"Watch out," he said sharply. "One more."

"That's the little one that we saw the first time the shadows attacked," Tahlia said.

The shadow flew past Marius, its movement erratic,

as if it was afraid. It flew into the boulder beside the one Fara was leaning on and bounced backward, trembling.

Ragewing roared at the varjuline, and the shadow cowered low.

"I have heard of too dumb to live," Trevain said, looking down his nose at the shadowling, "but too dumb to die is a new one, I must admit."

Marius lifted a hand and Ragewing let out a quick blast of fire. The small varjuline disappeared into the mossy ground. Trevain pursed his lips like he was disappointed in the shadowling.

Tahlia knelt beside Fara and smoothed the blanket so that it lay just under her chin. "Marius brought out his rich fellow's blanket for you, Fara. Soon, you and I will have enough to buy one of these too. I mean, come on. Don't die before we get paid, all right?"

Eyes burning from unshed tears, she tucked her friend's hair behind her ear. Golden boils showed over Fara's right eyebrow and along her cheek. She wasn't as pale as earlier, but she still hadn't opened her eyes or uttered a word.

"I have never seen someone leave any of the fire cages, so I don't have any information about healing her. It's not the same as the plague that killed me. This is the plague wrought by Katk and his first champion, the plague set on those with Mistgold blood."

Tahlia tried to get Fara to drink from her waterskin, but the liquid only spilled over her unmoving lips.

"Tell us the whole story, spirit," Tahlia said. "We need to know everything."

"How about I show you?" Trevain waved his hand and everything disappeared.

CHAPTER 21
MARIUS

The world flickered back to life. Marius spun, unsheathing his sword. Fully leafed oaks swayed in the breeze, and maples spread their branches along a well-set roadway of light stone.

They were not where they had been.

"What magic is this, spirit? Where are we?" He knew he shouldn't have trusted that Trevain fellow.

"Where is Fara?" Tahlia asked.

Tahlia was panting and wide-eyed with anxiety. Marius longed to grab her and hold her tightly. But of course, he couldn't or she would die. He remembered Ophelia's words in painful detail.

"Be calm, my lady," Trevain said, making Marius want to shake him. "Fara remains nearby, but not exposed to this dimension. You are in a version of my memory."

He looked very pleased with himself that he had brought them there.

Marius glared. "Return us to our squire or suffer the consequences."

"Time doesn't pass in the living world while we are here. Calm yourselves," Trevain said.

"So nothing is going to happen to Fara?" Tahlia asked, looking to Marius.

Marius gave her a shrug and focused on the spirit.

Trevain shook his head. "She must have some blood that isn't heavily Mistgold."

"Yes, she has a dash of human blood. Not like my level of the stuff, but a little," Tahlia said.

Trevain raised his eyebrows and pursed his lips. "I never thought to see anyone escape the varjuline alive. But no, nothing will pass while we are here. She will never even know we have left and the world there is frozen, so to say, while we visit my memory. Now, welcome to my home, the way it was before the dragon riders invaded."

Marius blinked. "We are in the Kingdom of Spirits?"

"We are. About eight hundred years before the current period."

Tahlia whistled. "It's beautiful. Why did it turn into such a hellish place? What did the dragon riders do? Do you mean the Order of Mist Knights?"

"This was before they called themselves that, but in a way." His gaze cut Marius as surely as a blade. "I speak of the same families that those of the order come from, yes."

Marius kept his tongue. He had heard versions of this history, and in none of them did his predecessors seem innocent. No, indeed his people had forced their way into this land and he wasn't proud of what had happened after. He didn't blame Trevain for his glare or the sharp tone of his words. But that was all the more reason to wonder why the ghost was helping them. He hated the order. Why was he giving them aid?

The verdant forests and lush farmlands shimmered until the group stood on a high hill overlooking a walled city crafted of massive rectangular stones.

"This was our capital. The jewel of our land." Trevain jabbed Marius with a scowl. "Your kind flew here and stripped our king and queen's coffers of silver and gold. Then you moved on to our mines, our livestock, our wild animals, and so on. While you were pillaging and doing exactly as you pleased, you spread a terrible plague."

Trevain lifted his ghostly fingers in a circular movement. Rubbish piled up along the city's streets and rats ran from building to building. The city's inhabitants and those traveling outside the walls were dotted with dark splotches. Their skin looked papery and rough.

"One of us decided to sacrifice all and raise a monster," Trevain said. "Some say he accessed Unseelie power."

The Unseelie Fae lived in another realm entirely. Though the current Unseelie king had ties to Marius's king—Seelie Fae King Lysanael—the two civilizations never crossed. Only the royals visited one another and only rarely.

Trevain continued his tale. "Others claim the monster was a summoned demon. No one knows the truth. What we do know is that this male, a guild master from my neighborhood, killed his wife and slowly bled himself to death. In the wake of his offering, a giant climbed out of the earth."

A three-story structure on the western edge of the city trembled, dust lifting from its walls and thatched roof. A dark gray-green hand exploded from the thatch, followed by a massive head and body. A giant stood up, the building crumbling to ruins around him while screams erupted from the diseased masses. The monster had glittering golden eyes and just the look of him turned Marius's stomach. It wasn't that he was hideous and frightening. He was, but the true horror came from the fact that the giant felt familiar somehow.

Why in all the hells would a monster feel familiar to him? He had never once seen this creature.

The giant stepped over the castle walls and grabbed a Green-flanked Terror and his rider. The dragon went limp and colorless. As the monster flung the rider to the ground, the rider's scream went silent and golden boils popped up along his face and arms. These new boils were like a strange mimic of the black spots on the natives of the kingdom.

Trevain waved his hand and the kingdom faded into night. "The giant's plague took revenge on the dragon riders who had invaded. None of those with mostly Mist-gold blood survived. Once the giant succeeded in his champion's task, the task set on him by the guild master, he returned to sleep beneath the ground."

Tahlia grimaced. "High Captain, I believe you have seen the bones of this giant."

"I have, yes."

"Oh, wait." Tahlia pointed at Marius. "Your hands were dirty after you woke up. Remember?"

"Yes."

"I bet you returned to the bones while we were sleeping."

"This damned curse." Marius stilled. He had spoken of something roughly related to his curse. The curse hadn't halted his tongue. "I am cursed." He stared at Tahlia. "I can say it. I am cursed."

"What do you mean?" Tahlia stepped closer.

He backed up, holding out his hands. "Stay away. If you touch me, you die. Ophelia set this curse on me and I haven't been able to utter a word about it to you."

His throat grew dry and tight and his heart pounded heavily in his chest like he was sick, but he was telling her. Finally!

"Marius..." Tahlia's beautiful eyes glistened and she tilted her head. "I knew you wouldn't just shut me out for no reason."

"I didn't realize this would affect your curse in this way," Trevain said. "I guess because we are here and removed from the living world, you are temporarily free of the curse set on you by Katk's new champion."

Tahlia faced Trevain. "So Katk is the giant? What does *champion* even mean?"

"The one who raises him is his champion. Stories say that his champion may ask for one act of dark magic, but then Katk will feed on those with Mistgold blood until he is satiated or until he runs out of victims."

"That means Ophelia is his champion. But how? The monster was never on Dragon Tail Peak," Marius said.

"We would have heard of that. My family and all of the riders' families would have been killed by his plague. I wouldn't be here if he had traveled into our region."

Trevain continued. "The ritual can most likely work from far away. And the standing stones and their runes keep Katk trapped here. There is some mystery as to how my people persuaded him to sleep again, but it has to do with Mother Twilight."

"Wait, wait, wait," Tahlia said. "I can only handle so much folklore and reminiscing for one afternoon. First, I want to hear more about Marius's curse."

Her gaze shot to his face, and her eyes held so much hope. Gods, he wanted to kiss her senseless. Breathing out, he focused on the problem at hand.

"So Ophelia truly raised the monster with dark magic." He shook his head. Despite the topic, his face stretched into a smile and the sensation was odd. "It's wonderful being able to speak about it. The curse held my tongue until now, it seems. But yes, Ophelia was in my rooms when I returned there after hearing about the commander's death. She rose and touched my mouth with a bloody finger. She said if I touched you, you would die. Much of my time since that moment has been foggy and dreamlike."

"More like a nightmare."

"Indeed."

"So you believe Ophelia had something to do with her father's death? Like what I was getting at when I found you and spoke to you? Do you even remember that?"

"I don't remember, but yes I do think she had something to do with the death. The ritual demanded blood and she used his."

Trevain was nodding. "Katk will be drawn to Ophelia just as you, her victim, are likely drawn to Katk."

Marius swallowed. His mind whirled with the cascading effects of the new commander of the order being the murderer of the previous. How could she bring herself to kill him? Madness. Such a mad tragedy. "I'm surprised Ragewing permitted this journey. He knew I wasn't in my right mind."

"Oh!" Tahlia smacked Marius's shoulder, her excited eyes changing to show wide-eyed terror.

She dropped back and stared at her fingers, whatever she had been about to say apparently forgotten.

And she had touched him.

"No…" Marius couldn't breathe. He turned to stare down Trevain. "How will the curse affect her? She only touched my clothing. Does that mean nothing will happen?" And that the love of his life wouldn't die before his eyes? "Don't even try your sarcasm or wry words with me right now, ghost, or I will find a way to end you."

"Calm yourself, knight. I would do no such thing," Trevain said to Marius. Then he turned toward Tahlia. "And you seem well enough."

Trevain appeared completely unruffled, which, of course, ruffled Marius greatly.

Marius eyed Tahlia's cheeks and bare forearms, watching for signs of anything deathlike. "Come now, spirit! You must know."

"She would turn to ash most likely. That's how most

curses work, don't they? How do you feel?" Trevain asked Tahlia.

"Fine." She looked up at Marius and an ache spread across his chest. Reaching out her unscathed fingers, she said, "Should we try again? Skin to skin?"

Marius drew away, heart tapping madly. "Absolutely not. Are you a fool?"

"A fool for you." Tahlia smiled, a twinkle in her beautiful eyes.

Trevain shrugged. "I don't think you would suffer any foul consequences. Although, I will say, you two are using my traumatic memory realm for your selfish purposes. I can't say that I appreciate it."

"I don't give a whit what you appreciate, spirit," Marius spat out. "We must understand what rules to follow to beat Ophelia and her monster at their game."

"Well, I suppose that does make sense," Trevain said.

Tahlia was suddenly gripping Marius's hand. He glared down at her, fear stabbing him repeatedly and making his eyes hot.

Please don't take her from me, Old Ones. If you ever cared for this rider, please refrain.

"Are you, how do you, Tahlia, I..."

Tahlia grinned again and the stabbing terror halted. "I'm great!"

Marius crushed her in his arms and pressed his lips to hers. The feel of her soft mouth on his and the curve of her against him nearly had him throwing her to the ground to ravish her properly.

"Still here," Trevain said.

"Still don't care," Marius said, taking a second away from Tahlia's lower lip.

Tahlia laughed against his mouth and drew her tongue across his. His body jolted with a desire stronger than anything he'd felt in his entire life. He wanted to shelter this female, to destroy anyone who dared to threaten her, to join with her in every physical and spiritual way possible.

He smoothed a hand across her cheek and delighted in the way she shut her eyes and sighed.

"Tahlia, you are not my knight right now. You are you. I am me."

Tahlia jumped up and wrapped her legs around him. He let out a surprised *"Oof,"* but he caught her neatly and secured her in his arms. Her warmth made him growl with want. *Mine, mine, mine*. His heart beat out the truth. She could be his mate if they both chose that path.

He kissed her hard, claiming her even though he wasn't ready to ask her out loud about their future. He was cursed. Until they solved that problem, no future existed for them. Tahlia returned the kiss, her sweet tongue curling over his and her fingers digging into his upper arms, where the vest ended and his softer tunic began. She rolled her hips against him and he gritted his teeth as longing flowed through him, deep and sure and wild.

But the wind rushed around them. The memory world's green forests and haze of long ago slipped away.

They were thrust back into the current world. An invisible force blasted Tahlia away from him. Marius tumbled, nearly ramming into Ragewing's front talons.

He sat up to see Tahlia on the ground beside Fara, Tahlia's face slack with shock.

The memory world was gone and they had returned to the current state of things. Marius shook his head to clear it and adjusted his trousers. Tahlia seemed alive and well. Gods, he worried she'd be hurt. They never should have risked touching.

"I'm fine, Marius," Tahlia said, standing up and brushing herself off.

Trevain was shouting nonsense and pointing.

"Gods, what is it, spirit? Must you shriek like a frightened hen?" Marius got to his feet.

"I saved Tahlia just now, so you can offer thanks, High Captain," Trevain snapped. "Now, look to the East!"

Katk, the plague monster, walked across the old road, smashing trees and driving boulders into the earth.

CHAPTER 22
TAHLIA

The giant stalked across the landscape with varjuline curling around his legs like scary little shadow puppies. Tahlia shivered, then stood, brushing herself off.

"Marius?" Tahlia looked him up and down, watching for signs of the curse's control.

His face only showed every emotion that she too was experiencing. Want. Fear. Confusion. Desperation.

"Lady Tahlia." He also looked exhausted.

"You're still yourself?" she asked. "Tell me your favorite game to play with Titus."

"I don't think the c—" He swore and snarled, looking away. He seemed to hate it when he lost his temper, like he was frustrated not only with the curse but with his reaction to it.

"Right." Tahlia nodded. "You can't say curse or anything related again."

The giant lifted its ugly, gnarled head and roared.

"At least, he's a ways off?" Tahlia said, her tone

forcibly hopeful. "Where is he headed?" As long as it wasn't toward them, that was fine for now. They still had to rouse Fara and figure out a plan. Gods, she needed some time to process what Marius had told her, Trevain's story, and, of course, the whole *plague monster who kills dragon-riding Fae is back* situation.

Trevain floated above the dying fire, just beside Fara, who still slept. "I have a guess and I don't like it."

Marius knelt beside Fara and felt for a pulse in her neck. "Speak plainly, spirit." He glanced up at Tahlia, a world of frustration and pain pinching his handsome eyes and mouth. "She is strong. I believe she is healing."

"Katk might have figured out that the standing stones are what trapped him here during his first waking period," Trevain said. "If he destroys them, he will be free to continue setting his revenge plague on Fae with Mist-gold blood from here to the coast."

"Why?" Tahlia asked.

"When the victims succumb to his plague, their blood and life force feed him. That is the only way he can remain awake."

"So to put him back to bed like the naughty fellow he is, we must starve him of victims?"

"That, or whatever solution the goddess, Mother Twilight, has up her proverbial sleeve. Perhaps we should find her..." He scratched his chin. "Presenting him to his champion would work if said champion breaks the magic that woke him."

Tahlia scowled. "Why would his champion put him to rest?"

"Supposedly," Trevain said, "if the champion did not

sacrifice himself or herself, the monster's reign will end when he sees the champion. Perhaps as a check on the magic's power, set by the Old Ones? No one truly knows. Only my fellow spirits whisper this truth and most of them are stark-raving mad."

Marius grumbled something unintelligible. "I don't know why you'd expect a situation like this to make sense. In my experience, dark magic follows no logical course. It's painfully undisciplined."

"That's such a Marius thing to say." Tahlia looked to Trevain. "What happens with Marius's curse in all of this?"

Trevain shrugged. "I would assume his curse will end if we manage to put Katk to sleep again."

A frown tugged at Tahlia's lips. "Assume?"

"The monster has only risen once," Trevain said sourly, rolling his eyes.

"Watch your tone, spirit," Marius snapped.

Pleasure coursed through Tahlia's body, warming her from head to toe. She smiled at Marius and was rewarded with a smile back.

"Forgive me," Trevain said to Tahlia.

Tahlia waved him off and knelt beside Fara. Her eyes opened. Red lines crisscrossed the whites and her lids were swollen. Tahlia exhaled in a rush and hugged Fara fiercely. She was as limp as a rag doll as Tahlia helped her lean back again.

"I'm so glad you're not dead," Tahlia said.

"Me too." Fara attempted to sit up once more, but she couldn't quite manage it.

"Don't get up. Not yet."

Fara nodded and relaxed, letting her eyes drift shut again. "I thought that was it for me."

"We all did," Trevain said, giving Fara a kind smile.

The experience with the memory realm had exhausted Tahlia and Marius, so they decided to rest if only for an hour or two. They asked Trevain to keep an eye out and every living being, dragons included, lay down to close their eyes for a short break.

"You're certain we can take the time to rest? He is going to be tough to catch," Tahlia said, looking in the direction Katk was headed.

"The dragons will outmatch his pace without much difficulty if they have a moment to rest," Marius said, the confidence of many years in the order making his words firm and his tone sure.

Giving him a thumbs up, Tahlia lay beside Fara and fell asleep watching her friend's purple eyelids flutter in dreams. She hoped they were dreams, anyway, and not nightmares.

A DRAGON SNOUT WOKE TAHLIA, and when she opened her eyes, Lija was staring down at her.

CHAPTER 23
TAHLIA

Tahlia and Marius readied for flight, adjusting saddles and checking bags and ties. They worked in silence to let Fara sleep a little longer.

A cough from Fara turned Tahlia around from where she'd been checking Lija's girth strap. Fara sat up, blinking.

"Feeling better?" Tahlia asked.

"I am. Yes. Well, maybe."

Tahlia brought her a skin of water. "You were right about the plant and the dragons. I ate some of the leaves and now Vodolija can communicate with me." Tahlia tapped her temple.

Fara's face lit up as she looked at Tahlia. "Really?"

Tahlia nodded. "Yes!"

Fara drank a healthy amount and handed the skin back to Tahlia. Her sluggish movements gave away the lingering fatigue of her experience.

Beside Ragewing, Marius frowned and grew still. His

hands were poised over one of his smaller satchels. "What are you two talking about?"

Another cough shook Fara, and she seemed to have forgotten about Marius's question. "We are leaving now, right? We have the High Captain, I see. Insane mission accomplished." She faced Marius. "Are you cursed? Did you break it?"

Marius grunted, and his jaw muscles worked.

"He can't tell us," Tahlia said, "but yes, he is, and no, we didn't. We still have a lot of things to do here before we can leave."

Tahlia looped an arm around Fara and helped her to stand. She was steady enough and Tahlia was thrilled to see it.

"I'm guessing these aren't tasks I'm going to be happy about," Fara said.

Tahlia smiled. "Definitely not."

"Why are you dragon riders so enamored with creative ways to end yourselves?"

Marius's lips tilted up for a second, and Tahlia's heart soared to see him doing so well. Was the curse easing off of him because Katk was awake and Marius had done as Ophelia's monster required by digging up his bones?

Trevain introduced himself to Fara and spent a few minutes filling her in on all the happenings while Marius and Tahlia tended to Ragewing's and Lija's old injuries.

"Trevain reminds me of someone," Tahlia said.

Marius raised an eyebrow. "Who?"

"I'm not sure. His face just looks like someone I know. It's odd."

Marius frowned, and Tahlia shrugged as she finished

corking the unguent Fara had brought. She placed the leather-wrapped bottle in one of the saddlebags.

Don't forget to have him eat the plant, Lija said.

"Ah! Right. Thanks."

"Who are you talking to?" Marius scowled and looked from Tahlia to Trevain and Fara.

Fara walked over on slightly unsteady feet and Lija bent so she could climb on. Tahlia and Marius each gave her a hand up.

"Wait here," Tahlia said to Marius.

She searched the ground until she found some of the blood-red plant. She plucked a bit and handed it over to Marius, careful not to touch him.

His lip lifted, showing his teeth.

"Shh, you're fine," she said, "and I'm fine. I know not to touch you. Now, eat that."

"Why would I?" Marius demanded.

"Because I told you to." Tahlia winked.

Fara and Trevain laughed. Marius grunted unhappily, but he shoved the plant into his mouth and chewed. His furrowed brow cleared. His mouth fell open.

"Ragewing?" he said quietly.

"Fara and Lija introduced me to this plant," Tahlia explained. "It sparks the ability for riders to hear their bonded dragons."

Marius faced Ragewing and had a hurried conversation, then Marius went silent though he still focused on his Heartsworn. He spun to face Tahlia. "But we can't speak back inside our minds?"

"We can. But it's not easy."

It is worth practicing, though, yes? Lija said.

"Definitely. Lija said we should practice and see if we can manage it after a while."

The effects should last forever. Once the talent blossoms, it remains. The plant is rare. It only grows in this land. My forefathers once lived here, hidden deep under the land's surface, where the sea flowed through secret caves.

"That is amazing."

"I'm jealous of this new thing," Fara said. "I'll be the big person and admit it."

"Why aren't you stelling me we are going to die from eating it? I'm impressed you're merely fretting over my friendship with Lija and how it might affect ours. Which it won't."

They took off into the sky, heading in the direction Katk had gone. Clouds whisked by, the air cold and sickly sweet with Katk's disgusting odor.

"Firstly, I'm not shouting warnings because I researched the plant. That's why I even bothered to tell you about it. Its effects on Fae are established and I have that information. Secondly, well, this is all just too much," Fara said. "Once you've hit this level of emergency, there is little point in warning everyone. We all know it's likely that death is about to greet us. Will we end up like you, Trevain?"

"I don't know. I suppose it's possible, but I died from the natural plague the Mistgold Fae brought. Your kind."

"Easy, ghost," Fara said. "Don't throw accusations at me. I wasn't alive back then. Not even close. I might be half dead, but I'm more alive than you and I can find a way to teach you manners." She cracked her knuckles.

This time, Tahlia had put Fara in the saddle's main

seat. She didn't want her friend falling and it was easier to keep a hold on her from the back.

"Also, why is everyone so mean to Trevain?" Fara asked. "I'm ecstatic you're here and helping us," she said to the ghost. "Without you, we would be clueless."

Trevain glowed brightly and lifted his chin, his ghostly robes fluttering in the wind. "Thank you, Lady Fara."

"Are you secure there, Lady Tahlia?" Marius called out in his Mistgold Fae voice. It echoed in her ears like drums and she bit her lip, loving the power behind it. She would save him. Somehow.

Trevain streamed along between the dragons. "You will most likely die of the revenge plague and I've seen no ghosts of those who suffered that fate."

Katk's stone-and-moss-colored head came into view over a tumble of high hills. The stench was overpowering.

CHAPTER 24
TAHLIA

"Gods save us from the smell," Fara said, adding on some elaborate noises. "I might perish from the stink before he has a chance to bespell me with any sort of disease."

"You hover here," Marius ordered, his whip already out and ready. "I'll circle him to get his attention."

"Explain to me why isn't Marius considered the monster's champion," Fara said.

Trevain nodded "Because though he dug up the bones, he didn't perform the ritual of blood sacrifice. Sounds like your Ophelia did that."

"She is not *our* Ophelia," Tahlia said. "We loathe that dog's arse."

Fara snorted. "You're demeaning dogs with that statement."

"True," Tahlia agreed. "She is worse than that. A damn nightmare with a pretty face."

Ragewing was a scarlet blur ringing Katk's massive skull. The snap of Marius's whip echoed off the rocky outcroppings along the hills. A roar blasted through the air and Fara covered her ears.

Careful now, Lija ordered as she tilted to one side, keeping Fara in the saddle.

Tahlia grasped Fara, bracing her friend between her arms as she held the low-profile pommel. The reins pressed into the skin between her fingers. Fara talked a big game, but she was trembling.

Katk reached toward Marius, but Ragewing shot into the higher clouds, disappearing from view.

Tahlia tapped Lija's neck and the Seabreak flew closer to Katk and flapped her four wings to hover. She blew one short blast of bright flame, the heat brushing over Tahlia's forehead as the wind rose.

The monster turned to face them, his eyes black holes of nothingness and his hands encircled in shadow and golden magic.

Fara shuddered. "Can we please fly away now very quickly?" she said, stuttering.

"Lija, fly!"

The dragon took off just as Ragewing exploded from the high clouds to fly beside them. They dashed toward the ruins, where the scent of Fara and the rest of them might keep Katk busy searching for victims. The trick would be to get him hooked on the blood under the ruins' broken great hall while they flew off.

They soared over the ruins and Katk stopped, sniffing the air.

He is taking the bait.

"I hope so."

The monster lifted its head and grabbed for Lija. Fara

screamed and Tahlia held tightly to her as the Seabreak dodged Katk's dark green fingers. Tahlia grew dizzy with the horrible smell and the fear of his touch.

"If he even grazes your flesh..." Trevain flitted away to float beyond the old castle's outer wall.

Ragewing dove toward Katk and blew fire.

"Here, monster!" Marius snapped his whip over the creature's bulbous ear.

Katk swung around, smashing through what remained of the great hall's floor. His bare—and fully disgusting—foot was covered in blood from one of the varjuline's ritual bowls. He grabbed the bowl, and the blood spilling from the container disappeared. The blood on his foot and ground did too.

Fara whimpered. "What kind of bizarre and horrifying thing is happening here? We are definitely going to die."

Tahlia shut her eyes and thanked the Old Ones that Fara was back to her old self. "I'm guessing that's one way in which he eats."

"Ew."

Lija shot into the sky, catching up with Ragewing, and they flew away from Katk.

THEY LANDED, deciding that everyone needed some rest if they were to keep on battling Katk. Fara had fallen asleep the moment her head hit her bedroll. Trevain had claimed to have ghost business elsewhere and he'd disappeared, leaving the dragons, Marius, and Tahlia on their own.

The fire's golden light danced across Marius's proud nose and strong cheekbones. Tahlia had never known she'd be envious of light.

"What are you thinking about?" Marius asked, his voice quiet enough not to carry to where the dragons gathered beside a sleeping Fara at the second fire.

Tahlia didn't want to say what she had been thinking. It would only be torture, and as much as she enjoyed giving him trouble, this time, teasing didn't feel right. Taking a swig from the flask of lavender mountain liquor Fara had brought, she drummed up a new question. Gods, the liquor was awful.

"What's your ideal day?" she asked finally.

He looked up, an almost comical frown on his face. "I'm sorry?"

Shrugging, she plucked a piece of long grass and twisted it around her finger. "You heard me. I was just curious."

"Always so curious."

His features softened, and she looked away, his tenderness burning her heart and soul. Their situation was such a wreck.

"Tea before dawn," he said. "A book in my hands and a day of flying ahead of me."

It was mad how hard she was falling for this male. "Tea and a book? I didn't expect that."

His eyebrows lifted. "How about you?"

"Guess."

His gaze snagged on her face, the look in his eyes bracing. "You only want to be in the sky. As much as you are able. You live to fly."

Her heart danced at how well he already knew her. "Exactly."

"But you don't mind landing long enough to have some cake."

A laugh bubbled from her. "True."

"Ask me anything, Tahlia."

Her breath caught. The way he said her name... "I don't have a list like some people." She gave him a pressing look. "So I'll have to think on it."

"What were you *really* thinking when I first asked you?" he asked. "Because that was a lie."

She swallowed. "Touching you."

Glancing away, he poked at the fire with a long stick. His throat moved in a swallow, his skin brushing the collar of his vest. Tahlia wanted to tuck her head into that space and press her lips to the beat of his pulse.

"Marius, look at me."

"It's too difficult."

Tahlia blinked, watching him stir the fire as if his life depended on its heat.

"If I study the soft edge of your cheek," he said, his deep voice a low whisper, "the lift of your upper lip, the curve of your breast, your pert nose, I'll come undone... I... Tahlia, this situation will kill me if it doesn't kill you."

She could hardly talk around the tightness in her throat. "We will break your curse."

"I wish I was as sure as you."

"We will find this Mother Twilight goddess that Trevain mentioned. She'll help us."

"She is only a story told to us by a ghost," he said. "How do we even know if she still exists?"

"We have to hope."

"Telling myself to feel things doesn't make it happen."

"Doesn't it?" she asked. "Try telling yourself over and over and over. Hold to that like you hold my heart."

He finally looked up and met her gaze. The desperation in his stormy eyes sent a bolt of lightning down her body, hitting her heart and restarting it, then shooting heat to her core. She swallowed.

His focus snagged on her mouth. "Stop biting your lip. I can't handle it."

Surprise brought a quiet laugh out of her. "Really? Doing this—" she said, biting it again, "—does it for you?"

"Thoroughly."

She couldn't help but snicker.

"You find my pain humorous, do you?" A teasing tone lightened his words.

"I'm sorry," she said. "I shouldn't."

"You can't help yourself. Vexing me is your new favorite pastime."

"Guilty as charged."

His scowl broke into a grin like the sun rising after a long, cold night. The urge to leap over the fire and dive into his arms was so powerful that it actually hurt.

She grabbed the flask of lavender mountain horror and handed it to him. "Once we break this curse," she said as he took a swig, "I'll show you exactly how much fun vexing can be." She ran her hand down her chest very, very slowly.

The splash of the drink on the ground had Marius

jolting out of a stupor. He straightened the flask and swore. "It's your fault I gave half of that to the earth," he said to her, his eyes smoking.

An idea popped into her head. "Why don't you follow me to that little copse of trees?"

Frowning, he did as requested.

This was going to be interesting.

They left Ragewing and Lija to their sleep, then Marius and Tahlia walked to the small cluster of maples, oaks, and pines.

The slender shadows of the wood welcomed them, the wind scented with something that was fairly pleasant. Moonflower maybe? Clover? Definitely pine.

Tahlia's stomach fluttered at what she was about to suggest. What would he say?

CHAPTER 25
TAHLIA

She stopped and leaned back on a tall, wide maple—one of the only large trees in the area. He halted a few paces back, keeping his distance for her safety. She hated that space between them with a super searing type of hate.

The light through the trees made his Fae-white hair shimmer like magic from the ancient worlds, like Unseelie magic. Marius was every bit as dangerous as an Unseelie. He could snap her neck in a breath.

"Why are you grinning like that? It's...not a comforting expression, let me tell you."

She snickered. "I like how deadly you are."

He tilted his head and lifted one moonlight-hued eyebrow. "You do, hmm?"

That deep voice sent wonderful shivers down her back. She licked her lips and noticed that his gaze focused on the movement of her tongue.

"Just why did you drag me into the haunted forest, little salty?"

"I'm not sure I love that nickname."

"Lady of the Skies?"

"Maybe one is good for a certain situation and the second for another, very different scenario."

"Ah. I will have to study your preferences once we are free of..." His lips tightened and his throat moved in a swallow.

"For now, let's say your hands do as mine do."

His brow furrowed but he held up his hands, palms toward the forest's canopy as if in surrender.

Tahlia chuckled, slid her hand down her hip, and cupped one side of her own arse. She winked.

His lips pulled into a smile and he seemed ready to chuckle, the light dancing in his stormy eyes. He mimicked the movement, grabbing his backside and smirking at her.

"It's my turn now. It's only fair," he said.

Tahlia's toes curled inside her boots. "All right, then. Let's see what you've got."

Marius's near grin fell away and his eyes narrowed as he studied her face. He lifted a hand and drew his fingers from his temple to his jaw. She echoed his hand's action, her heart beating soft and slow now. He set his hand against his cheek. She did as well and turned her face into her hand slightly, leaning into the touch. It was her flesh, but the intention was his. A shadow of a smile graced his mouth.

"You're so lovely, Tahlia. I never tire of looking at you. The way you smile. How your forehead wrinkles when you're thinking..."

He shifted his hand to slide over the spot between his

eyebrows, and so she did the same, shutting her eyes for just a moment to pretend he could touch her again. To imagine they were like any couple in the Realm of Lights, courting and unrestrained.

"My turn," she said, feeling strangely shy.

She opened her eyes and set her hand against her heart. He placed his hand over his chest and he curled his fingers for a moment like he wanted to grip his heart. She drew a line from her chest to the hollow in her throat. Her pulse beat quickly beneath her fingers. Marius slid his hand up too and a sweet smile pushed at his lips. The heat of a tear trickled down Tahlia's cheek. Marius lifted his hand and brushed his cheek as if he could wipe her tears away.

"I love you, Tahlia. You know that, right? I assume you already have me figured out."

Her heart leapt and rolled and a broken laugh of joy fell from her mouth. "I had hoped. I love you too, Marius. Even if I'm not supposed to."

"That just makes it more fun for you."

She knew they were ignoring the curse for now and that he meant the fact that she was half-human and their relationship could cause further disturbances in the order.

"I do like a challenge," she said, wiping her tears away with the back of her hand and adding a teasing note to her voice.

She met his gaze and let her eyes show him that it was time to play a little more, to stop the weeping, to enjoy one another if only for this brief moment. He smiled in return, his glance going dark and hot. Want simmered low in her belly and she took a shuddering breath.

Smoothing her palm down between her breasts, she lifted an eyebrow. He mimicked the movement, his lips parting slightly and his fully slitted irises going wide.

"I'm taking over now," he said.

The growl of command in his voice made her skin flush. He continued down his torso, then swept upward to palm his chest. He drew a thumb back and forth. She did the same, inhaling quickly as the touch had her nipple rising beneath her tunic and vest. Tilting his head as if he was truly enjoying the view, he ran his hand down to cup himself. Tahlia swallowed, her face on fire and her body melting. He was very obviously enjoying this now.

With a painfully slow movement, he stroked himself and she did likewise. The pull toward him was nearly overpowering. She wanted him against her, overwhelming her in all the best ways. Marius's hand shifted into a faster pace. Her blood going molten, she obeyed his unspoken order. She leaned back on the tree, panting as release coiled inside her.

With his free hand, Marius dragged his fingers across his mouth. Tahlia did the same but nibbled her forefinger in the process. She sucked it between her lips and he growled, his eyes shuttering for a moment. He reduced the speed of the hand at his cock, and she whimpered quietly, not wanting to slow down. Her release was building, pounding in her blood, making her knees weak. Vicious, he was, as he eased into a crawling pace. He wore a wicked grin. She wanted to lick him up and down; her lips ached with the need to taste his skin again.

"Faster, Marius, please..."

His tongue darted out to wet his lips and he increased his pace little by little. She mimicked him perfectly even as her body demanded more, more, more. Finally, her body uncoiled and shivered. Pleasure jolted through her, and he shuddered, uncovering himself momentarily.

They gasped together, and he grinned at her.

"You are the true monster in this haunted kingdom because now I only want you more," he said.

"Goes both ways, my scary, lovely captain."

"I'll be right back," he said. "You take all the time you need to gather yourself."

"Thanks."

He pressed his fingers to his lips, kissed them, then held them out toward her. She touched her mouth, feeling the smile he'd placed there. After a quick trip back to the fireside, Marius returned with the flask. They stood under the trees, drank, and talked about little nothings that meant everything.

She would save him from this. Or she would die trying. Marius was hers and no one was going to take him from her.

CHAPTER 26
TAHLIA

Trevain led them to another forest, a sun-hued gathering of trees with wildly long and spindly leaves.

"My grandmother always said this was one of Mother Twilight's homes," Trevain said, "but I have never sought the goddess."

"She's a goddess?" Fara asked. "Why would she help us?"

Right. Fara had missed some information. "Yes, and why wouldn't she?" Tahlia asked.

"Perhaps because we are Mistgold Fae and we killed everyone with our germs?"

"I'm not Mistgold."

"Great. So she'll give you a big hug and strike the rest of us down with lightning. Fun plan."

"Hush. It'll be fine. Just you watch."

"If only we all had Tahlia's bright outlook on life," Marius said.

"It's going to get her killed," Fara said.

"Not if I have anything to do with it," Marius said.

"I'm still here, you know." Tahlia raised an eyebrow and Marius almost smiled. Every time his mouth lifted like that, her soul sang.

Trevain led them onward through the forest. The leaves were healthier here than elsewhere in this ruined kingdom, but no birds trilled as they should have, and Tahlia didn't think it was simply the presence of two dragons. The trees thinned in one spot and a waterfall splashed down from a sloping creek bed.

"It's beautiful." Tahlia set a hand on Lija.

The remnants of great power lie here like dust. She is not here.

"Lija says Mother Twilight isn't here," Tahlia said.

"She can tell?"

Marius looked to his dragon. He nodded and faced Tahlia, Lija, Fara, and Trevain. "Ragewing agrees. He said that she was here long ago but has traveled to another place. Trevain, what do you think?"

Trevain gasped. "You're asking me?"

The muscles around Marius's jaw flexed. "You have shown your trustworthiness thus far. I'm trying to take you at your word."

"I'm so honored," Trevain said, his tone wry.

"Watch it, ghost. My dragon is currently wondering if ghosts like you react to fire the way varjuline do."

Trevain seemed to shrink. "If you snuff me out, you'll have no guide."

"You aren't the only spirit wandering this land," Marius said.

"Enough, you two," Tahlia said. "Let's move on. Where to, Trevain?"

He led them onward for a while, the sky's mist wetting their faces and weighing down wings and Fae limbs.

A large cluster of lush pines stood out among the dark sludge of the valley and rolling hills. Within the first row of trees, a circle had been cleared. A perfect ring of space like an invisible door hung there suspended by unseen forces.

Trevain approached the circle slowly, holding out a hand and indicating everyone should halt. The dragons landed in the rocky area in front of the small forest, mud and algae splashing up their legs and cloaking their talons.

This place feels like being underwater.

"Really? In what way?"

It's difficult to explain in your tongue. Immersed in that which is not air. Held by forces outside your control.

"Interesting. Do you think the goddess is here?"

I would bet on it.

"Do dragons have a system of gambling?"

No. I was just using phrases you Fae use. Dragons are too wise to risk money on games.

"Right. Of course." Tahlia smirked up at Lija.

"Is the dragon telling you to hush? Because that is your move here, Mist Knight," Trevain whispered, raising a chastising eyebrow.

"Yes, Mother," Tahlia snarked back.

Trevain made a snarling face at her.

"Ragewing believes we should go in first and check

the area with Trevain," Marius said. "Lady Tahlia, you keep watch of Fara, and I will whistle when you should enter."

"Something about you whistling to get me to come like one calls a dog isn't making me smile, High Captain."

He gave her a flat look. "If this was a mission for the order, your comment would be ruled insubordination."

"I think we've established that when you dig up a giant ancient monster, boring rules like that go out the proverbial window."

He rolled his eyes. "I will shout for you, my lady. Does that please you?"

Trevain and Fara traded a laughing glance.

Lija's husky laughter floated through Tahlia's mind. The sound made her grin from ear to ear.

"That will be perfect. Thank you, Marius."

"I don't like this lapse in protocol."

"Go on, now. You can lecture me later."

Marius growled quietly and rode Ragewing to the edge of the strange cutout circle. Following Trevain's watery golden light, the Heartsworn lifted each leg carefully, stepping through to the green shadows of the wood.

He is right not to disturb the magical entrance, Lija said.
What would happen if he did?
I'm not certain, but I wouldn't want us to be nearby when it occurred. Did you realize you just spoke into my mind again?
I'm getting good at this! "Huzzah!"

Fara jolted against Tahlia, nearly toppling from Lija's back. Tahlia caught her and righted her in the saddle.

"Why are you screaming in my ear?" Fara demanded.

"I just spoke into Lija's mind again."

"No, you shouted. In my ear."

"No, before that. I said something else and Lija told me." Tahlia hugged Fara. "Isn't this telepathy thing wonderful?"

"If it involves less destruction of my eardrums, yes."

"Lady of the Skies!" Marius called out.

Tahlia waved.

"If we die here, at least you two had some time to flirt," Fara said.

"Ah, Fara. Be nice. We're about to meet a goddess. She could smite you down for that poor attitude."

"Fantastic. Now, I'm worried about smiting. What is that again?"

Tahlia patted her on the shoulder. "Quiet now, squire, and remember that coming along was your grand idea."

"Sometimes I loathe myself."

Lija brought them through the circle, her wings held tightly against her shimmering body. They caught up to Ragewing, Marius, and Trevain under a bower of red flowers growing in the branches of intertwined conifers. Petals flitted down in the breeze and the forest's scents lulled Tahlia into a relaxed state. Even Fara seemed to release some of the tension as she sat up in the saddle, straining to see past Ragewing. They walked slowly into a clearing that glowed with rainbow light.

In the center of the clearing, an old female sat on a stool.

CHAPTER 27
TAHLIA

The old woman's gnarled, glowing hands moved slow and sure as she knitted red woolen yarn. A few finished pieces lay folded at her hem on the mossy ground. Tahlia's breath caught at the beauty of the goddess. The weight of the goddess's presence was akin to the sensation of Marius's attention. Like a warm cloak had been draped across her shoulders and she'd downed a cup of crystal wine.

Tahlia glanced at Marius. Was his skin glowing slightly as well? She blinked and the sparkling of his cheeks and forehead was gone.

The goddess lifted her knobby chin and regarded the group with a pair of dark, luminous doe eyes. They were larger than a Fae's eyes and glossy like an animal's. The effect should have been frightening, but instead, only wonder poured through Tahlia's soul.

She slipped from the saddle, helped Fara down, then knelt beside Marius, who had also dismounted quickly.

Red petals floated down to land on Marius's shoulders. The petals caught in Tahlia's hair and snuggled into her palms like small creatures longing for a warm spot to take shelter.

"Good hearts, I greet you," the goddess said, her lips unmoving but her voice strong and clear. Her accent was not too different from Trevain's, with strewn-together consonants and slightly rounded vowels. "Come closer and we will talk."

Marius stood and turned, holding a hand out to Tahlia, less of a helpful task than a simple show of affection.

"Marius..." she started. He had forgotten the curse. She didn't blame him. The goddess's presence was enough to make one believe everything had been set to rights in all the realms.

He winced and nodded, withdrawing.

Trevain and Fara joined them, walking alongside Ragewing and Lija.

"Greetings, Mother Twilight," Trevain said. He kissed his palm, then pressed his hand to the ground near her feet.

Tahlia mimicked the show of respect, then Marius and Fara did as well. The dragons bowed their large heads, eyes shuttering in a display of trust.

Listen closely, my rider, Lija whispered into Tahlia's mind.

Oh, don't worry. I feel her power, too.

Good. I worried you might try to entertain her with your latest knock-knock joke.

Tahlia bit her lip to keep from laughing.

"You seek aid against Katk," the goddess said.

"Aye," Marius said. "Do you have advice for us?"

"You cannot fight him. Not truly. But you can trap the monster and take him to his champion. You must move quickly. If he leaves this kingdom, he will end all the Mistgold Fae."

But Ophelia was far beyond this cursed place. "His champion is in the Shrouded Mountains, in the land bordering this one."

"Then you must trap him tightly. You must be the one to do it," the goddess said to Tahlia.

"Because of my human blood?"

"Yes, little wise one. He will not seek to plague you. But if Katk creates more varjuline, they will cage you and drain you of blood and spirit to feed themselves. The varjuline are not picky about the blood they consume. They are more animal than Katk and have no reason, only instinct."

Marius frowned. "Katk has reason? He seems blind with rage and driven by his curse alone."

"He seeks to finish what his first champion started. It is his calling."

"What will happen when we bring him to his current champion?" Trevain asked.

"When Katk is released and in the presence of his champion, that soul alone may put him to sleep for good."

"And if she refuses?" Tahlia asked.

The goddess inclined her head. "Does she want to end the Mistgold Fae?"

"She is of that blood," Tahlia said.

"Ah. Then you see what will be her motivation to put him in the ground once more."

But Tahlia could just imagine Ophelia listening to them telling the story. She wouldn't believe them. She would hesitate. She would get them all killed.

An image of Tahlia standing on a field of bloodied bodies, both Fae and dragon, washed across her mind. She shivered.

The goddess tilted her head, studying Tahlia. "That is only one potential outcome."

With a pair of heron-winged bone scissors, the goddess cut the yarn, then rose and faced Tahlia. She held out the piece she'd been knitting, a length of red with braided tassels. "I made this for you, Weaver."

Palms sweating and still filled with petals, Tahlia stepped forward. The goddess tied the piece around Tahlia's hips. Sparks of magic and the lull of power cocooned Tahlia until the goddess shifted her weight and eyed the belt.

"It fits." Her dark eyes found Tahlia's. "Remember who you are here," she said, touching a spot near Tahila's heart. "Little doesn't mean lesser in your case. Cleverly made by the Fire, there isn't a piece of you that goes to waste. You are the Autumn Weaver."

"I'm what?"

Mother Twilight just smiled and tapped her chin. "When you wear this belt, you are stronger than Katk. Not in the way of hand or foot, but in the ways that matter more."

She was lovely and powerful, but perhaps not the

best at practical information. "Thank you very much, goddess. How exactly do I go about trapping Katk?"

"You will know."

The clearing turned to darkness.

CHAPTER 28
TAHLIA

When the light came again, they were back on the other side of the strange circle cut into the forest.

They stood side by side, dragons, ghost, and Fae, all seemingly stunned to the same degree. Tahlia touched the woven belt at her waist. The wool was soft like any other wool. Did this thing truly have power of some sort?

Tahlia turned to Marius, who stood on the other side of Trevain. "Why wouldn't she just tell me what to do?"

"I assume—" he started, trying to see Tahlia clearly around the ghost. Then he let out a small snarl and waved at Trevain, shooing him away. Trevain gave Marius a look but allowed Marius to usher him a few steps back.

Marius's broad chest moved as his gaze slid over Tahlia's face. The urge to touch him nearly overwhelmed her.

"As I was saying, Mother Twilight most likely knows we must go through an ordeal to gain the abilities we need to succeed."

"I'm game." Tahlia rubbed her hands together, excited for the next step in this grand adventure. "Any task that will stop that giant from killing everyone on the mountain and," she said, lowering her voice, "any ordeal that will get my hands back on you, I'm more than willing to conquer."

"I have no doubt you will subdue Katk, Lady of the Skies. But you must learn to hold your tongue when we are back with the order, on missions and in training. You must learn a semblance of discipline regarding our relationship and the order." His eyes softened and heated, his warmth extending from his muddied leathers to brush over her body.

"Aye, High Captain. I will behave. Mostly."

He chuckled and shook his head.

"You know, you look even better all grimed up like this," she said, gesturing to the dirt on his cheek, his tangled hair, and the mud along his white vest and trousers.

"I'm filthy."

"I understand that you hate it, but it does something for me seeing you ruffled."

"I'm well aware." His lips turned up at one side, and gods, did she want to kiss him until neither of them could breathe...

"What's the plan?" Fara called out. She was rubbing salve on Lija's scales like the wonderful person she was.

Marius saw what Fara was up to and seemed to be having a silent conversation with Ragewing.

"Did you figure out how to speak to him in your mind?" Tahlia asked.

"I did."

We should head toward the stones, Lija said.

A chill wrapped Tahlia. *Can you tell if Katk is headed there again?*

Yes. His evil energy thrums from that direction, from the lands just before the old border.

"Lija says Katk is going for the stones again," Tahlia said. "Eh, where did Trevain go?"

Fara and Marius looked around, and Lija faced Ragewing, their gazes locking over everyone's heads.

"Ragewing says the spirit was pulled to another place," Marius said.

"What does that mean?" Fara asked, her voice getting high-pitched.

"He is a ghost. Who knows the mystery of his afterlife?" Marius said, apparently not at all concerned.

Tahlia mounted Lija. "What is your problem with him anyway? You're a little mean to the fellow."

"I'm a *little mean* to everyone or did you not notice?" His eyes sparked with humor.

"Well, yes, you're the King of Grumps, but you're more about discipline and doing what is right. You don't usually push at people the way you do with Trevain."

"I am trying to trust him, but the feeling wavers. The fact is, we don't know what his motivation is for helping us."

Once again, the familiar look of Trevain pushed at

Tahlia like a memory she couldn't quite grasp. "He can't just be a nice ghost?"

"His civilization was ruined by ours. So no, I think he has an ulterior motive, and though I can't blame him for that, I won't trust much of what he says until I figure him out."

Hurry, rider, Lija said.

"Should we move?" Tahlia asked Marius. She pushed her curiosity about Trevain away.

Marius gave a curt nod, and he climbed atop Ragewing in one seamless maneuver. She'd never tire of watching him do that.

They took to the sky with Fara in the saddle's extra seat behind Tahlia. Tahlia had Fara untie her quiver from the rest of the gear. Reins in her teeth, Tahlia slipped the quiver onto her belt, then took her bow from Fara's outstretched hand. She tucked the reins under an arm.

"Thanks!" she said to Fara over her shoulder.

"It's what I'm here for!" Fara sounded like she was about to throw up despite the forced cheer in her tone.

Tahlia nocked an arrow and watched the ground for Katk.

"So that goddess was vague, wasn't she?" Fara said. "*You will know.*" She wiggled her fingers.

"Yes, and what was all that about the Autumn Weaver? I like pumpkin cakes and bonfires as much as the next person, but I doubt that's what the goddess was going on about."

Fara shivered. "Probably something horrible you will have to fight."

"More horrible than a plague giant?" Tahlia asked.

"I'm endlessly surprised at the terrors that pop into your life."

"Glad I keep you on your toes."

Fara closed her eyes and sighed like Tahlia had drained her of every ounce of patience.

Marius and Ragewing led them over a valley rutted with old roads and the chewed-up remains of villages and walled towns. A river passed through the valley and ran into a quarry that reflected the dragons' shapes.

Katk's lumbering form filled the horizon.

Tahlia had to set her jaw to keep from calling out a warning that no one needed.

"Really hoping that wisdom shows up any second now," she said, more to herself than anyone else.

Fara squeezed Tahlia's shoulder. "You can do this. I can't. I will probably fall off Lija and perish. But you, you'll be fine."

"No perishing today, please."

"I wish Trevain was here," Fara said. "He knew things. He could have helped you here, I bet."

Tahlia agreed. "I hope he is all right. He's been wonderful, no matter what Marius says."

"Is he still worried about Trevain's motives?"

"Yes. The whole *ruining Trevain's civilization and killing everyone he knew* thing," Tahlia said.

Fara made a grumbling noise. "But that was ages ago. He didn't seem to be harboring a grudge, helping us the way he did."

"And that's why Marius suspects him. He was too helpful too fast."

"I'm starting to wonder if Marius is right," Fara said. "Maybe we truly are better off without Trevain."

Tahlia glared over her shoulder. "Don't you start too. Trevain is a sweetheart."

"Only you would call a ghost a sweetheart," Fara said.

Lija chuckled in Tahlia's mind.

Katk was near enough now that the stench of him brought their conversation to a halt.

"You take the lead on this," Marius called out over the roar of the monster.

Tahlia took a shuddering breath and touched the woven belt. But nothing came into her head. No ideas. Not anything resembling a plan. She had to stall.

But they had no time for that. Over the hill, the standing stones rose from the fog. Katk would be there in mere moments.

The monster swung a fist at Ragewing. The dragon blazed a full-force flame at Katk and he reared backward, dodging the fire.

A thought simmered deep in Tahlia's mind. She pushed the thought toward Lija.

Katk's shadowlings had used a cage of fire to hold Fara. Maybe that would work for Katk?

Good idea, rider, Lija said.

Glad to hear you think so. Tahlia took a steadying breath.

"Create a crescent of flame above him and we will slowly lower the elevation!" Tahlia shouted toward Marius. She prayed the dragons would have enough fire to make this happen.

"Aye!" Marius called out, his body leaning forward as Ragewing tilted upward to hover, wings flaring.

Lija, if Ragewing's fire dies, I need you to fill the crescent. Are you feeling up to this? We will have go to in close for the flames to touch and create a barrier.

We will rope him in like shepherds do to sheep. Don't doubt my fire, rider. I am here and I am ready to fight.

Lija flew close, Marius and Ragewing going in as well. If Katk reached up now, the plague would hit Marius or Katk's fist would simply smash Ragewing out of the sky. Neither sounded pleasant.

"Now!" Tahlia's throat was already raw.

The dragons blew fire and Katk wheeled left, trying to avoid the flame. The dual fires rippled through the air, hissing into the fog and sending waves of heat across Tahlia's face. Katk let out another ear-splitting roar. Ragewing's fire sputtered and went out. He and Marius dropped back and Lija shuddered as she increased her fire to make up for the loss.

Lija's body rippled under Tahlia, the vibrations making her teeth knock together. Tahlia shot three arrows in quick succession. The monster batted two away, but one stuck in the side of his neck. Gold and black poured from the wound, but Katk didn't stagger.

He must yield, Lija said, her voice in Tahlia's mind weakening and broken with effort.

Ragewing flew around behind Lija and Marius shouted, "Pull back! She's draining herself. Pull back!"

I'm not. Do not ask me to stop!

But the pain in Lija's voice pushed a cold dread through Tahlia's chest.

Lija, the High Captain has given us an order. We must. No, I can do this...

The fire sparkled and leapt erratically. In the space between one blast and the next, Katk swung his fist. His knuckles smashed into Lija's wing. Lija shrieked, an ear-cracking sound. They spun backward, completely out of control. Fara clutched onto Tahlia's waist. Tahlia could hardly breathe.

Ragewing shot beneath Lija. He stretched a wing and caught at her broken one, steadying her as the ground came at them fast. With Ragewing's help, Lija managed to even out in the air and soar to a stop.

Katk roared and stalked toward them. Fury burned in his demon eyes.

Ragewing and Marius whirled to face the monster.

Tahlia stood in the saddle and placed hands on Fara's shoulders. "Stay with her. Do what you can." She thrust her dagger, hilt first, at Fara, who stuttered something unintelligible and accepted the blade.

With her short sword still sheathed at her belt, Tahlia leapt from Lija's back to Ragewing's. Marius turned, eyes like bolts of lightning.

"What in the name of all the gods do you think you're up to?" he demanded.

Standing and doing her best to remain so while Ragewing lashed out at Katk with talons, she nocked an arrow. She aimed and fired. The arrow zipped past Katk's gnarled ear.

"Helping you not die," she said to Marius, her words a blur and her pulse leaping. "And I'm keeping that monster's hands off my dragon!"

Her second arrow glanced off Katk's rock-hard head and fell to the ground.

Ragewing kept fighting while Marius slung his whip through the air. The whip snapped across Katk's left eye and he howled. Blood poured from the injured eye, black and gold gore leaking down the monster's broad cheek. Katk surged forward and Ragewing was driven backward.

Tahlia tumbled to the mud beside Lija, who tried to breathe more fire at the monster but only managed a flurry of sparks. Tahlia scrambled for her dropped bow, snagged it, then she rolled and shot another arrow at Katk, this time toward his softer bits.

Katk dodged the arrow and hurried forward, his gaze on the standing stones.

They were losing him. Lija was down, maybe for good. Ragewing was out of fire. Sweat trickled down Tahlia's face and she swiped it away with the back of her sleeve. They couldn't lose this fight.

"Go!" she shouted at Marius, who was staring at her from Ragewing's back like he wanted to take her up with him.

The scarlet dragon took off like a bolt from a crossbow. Tahlia threw her bow down and drew her short sword. She ran after them, feet pounding over a rise of mossy rock. Ragewing flew in front of Katk's face and lashed the clawed tip of one wing across the monster's good eye. Tahlia couldn't see everything from the ground, but Katk certainly wasn't slowing. If anything, his steps were growing longer and more sure as he came within feet of the first rune-marked border stone.

Lija, stay with Fara. Don't try to join me.

Lija's only answer was a resounding roar that bounced off the wall of rock Tahlia ran beside. Tears pricked Tahlia's eyes. Lija's pain shadowed Tahlia's side like a varjuline had latched onto her arm and between her ribs.

Marius's whip cracked. Katk whirled, more graceful than he should have been at his size, and he reached toward Marius. Marius leapt from Ragewing's saddle and landed hard. His face shone with sweat as his sword flashed. Was his leg injured? Blood poured from Katk's knee. Ragewing flew at the monster, lashing out with talon and tooth, but Katk bent, dodging the scarlet dragon's attack. The monster swiped a hand at Marius.

Three thoughts hit Tahlia's mind like quick cuts from the sharpest blade.

Katk wasn't going to miss.

Marius would die cursed and plagued with golden boils—the same horrible end as many of his Mistgold ancestors.

She was the only one close enough to save him.

Her blood singing through her veins that this was her mate, she jumped between Katk's hand and Marius, her gladius outstretched like a spear's head. Katk's hand hit her. The blade sank into his foul flesh, and she held on to the hilt. The monster shook his hand to dislodge the blade. Tahlia was thrown into the air. Her stomach lifted as she fell again. Katk batted her body aside. She slammed into the earth. Her breath left in a violent gust. But she was on her feet before the pain hit her.

Marius stumbled backward as the monster grabbed

for him again. Tahlia reached out and shoved Marius back.

Their eyes met. Sorrow swallowed the storm of Marius's gaze. He mouthed one mournful phrase.

No, my heart, my love.

Katk bellowed, grabbed Tahlia, and lunged toward the standing stones.

A wave of aching pain started in Tahlia's palms, where she'd touched Marius. The sickening sensation spread into her chest, down her legs, and up her neck toward her face. A shiver ran through her. She was like an egg cracked against stone, her strength and energy spilling into Katk's sticky hold on her.

The curse crawled through her body. The monster held her tight. He stomped on the first of the standing stones and the rock exploded. A wind scented with green grass and rain touched her cheeks.

She shut her eyes. "Goodbye, Marius, Lija, Fara, and Ragewing. I'm sorry I failed."

A warmth circled her waist. She opened her eyes. Red sparks lit her torso, only partially visible within Katk's great hand. An image shimmered to life over the view of the second stone. Katk smashed the runed stone with a fist and threw Tahlia to the ground.

But the image only grew clearer.

Titus stood beside Maiwenn and Ewan. Claudia, Atticus, Justus, and Enora were there too. Then all of the riders except Ophelia. They weren't truly present though. This was only a hallucination.

Tahlia! Lija shouted into Tahlia's mind.

She realized Lija, Fara, and Marius had been shouting her name as they tried to fight Katk.

"Tahlia! Don't give up! Fight!" Fara's voice was a reedy plea on the wind in Tahlia's ears.

Blinking, she pressed a palm against her pounding forehead. The image of the other riders faded. The view of Katk's massive form and broken bits of the standing stones went black. Tahlia fell into darkness.

CHAPTER 29
MARIUS

Tahlia's head thumped against the muddy earth. Her body shook violently on impact. Panic ripped Marius's chest and his stomach churned. He climbed onto Ragewing's back, then helped Fara up and settled her in the saddle. Pale as a fading dragon lavender bloom, she didn't say a word. Ragewing would have to carry Lija and Tahlia too.

"Will you struggle to transport so many?" Marius asked Ragewing.

Stop fretting about me, Ragewing said into his mind.

I will not, Marius said. *You will be carrying us all. It's far too heavy a burden.*

We will rest along the way. I can do this, rider.

Marius prayed Ragewing wouldn't end up exhausted into death after this chase.

"Lift your arms, squire," Marius said quietly to Fara.

She obeyed, her movements sluggish. He ran his whip around both their waists so there was less of a chance Fara would fall during this difficult journey.

Marius's gaze strayed once more to Tahlia. Her eyelids were nearly purple and her mouth was slack.

Ophelia's curse had invaded her body. He'd known it the second she touched him because a cold unlike anything winter could dole out had nearly knocked him backward. It would kill her. Her death wouldn't be from plague as he or Fara would suffer if Katk got his hands on them, but the curse's own dark end. How long would she last? What could they do to save her?

Why did you do it, Tahlia?

He swallowed hard and tapped Ragewing's scales. The dragon lifted into the air.

Marius's mind twisted around her sacrifice, trying to comprehend why she had given herself for him. Didn't she grasp the fact that his life was a husk without her in it? She'd barged into his world and turned everything beautifully upside down.

With one of his taloned feet, Ragewing took gentle hold of Tahlia, then he gathered Lija around the middle. His wings beating an erratic rhythm and his scales heating under the press of Marius's hand, Ragewing launched into the sky.

The ground below showed evidence of Katk's flight. Some of the scant trees in the area had been crushed into the moss and mud. Footprints the size of Lija created a trail leading out of the Kingdom of Spirits and well into the farmlands of the Realm proper. A barn lay half-smashed and a crowd of folk ran down the king's road to the south.

And there was Katk in the distance, climbing along a foothill. He splashed down into a lake and waded through. Water rolled up and over the lake's edge to flood an inn that sat along the road.

Ragewing increased his speed, his sides heaving with the effort.

Marius gritted his teeth.

Damn you, Ophelia.

After they cleared the first of the true peaks, Marius tapped Ragewing, asking him to land and rest.

The dragon relented, the fatigue obvious in the way he panted and the labored movements of his wings. His head hung low as he circled a small clearing near one of Katk's footprints. Ragewing eased Lija and Tahlia to the ground first, then landed.

Marius untied Fara with a careful, quick movement, not wanting to startle her. She had started to shiver with shock. He dug in one of his bags and found an extra cloak. Pulling it around her, he spoke softly, trying to ease her heart with meaningless words of comfort.

"All will be well." The words tasted like something very close to a lie—so bitter that it puckered his tongue. Not even his deep mind believed they would come out of this without experiencing great loss.

He helped her from Ragewing's back. It was miraculous that both Lija and Ragewing had deigned to allow Fara to fly with them. Perhaps the fact that squires could not ride bonded dragons was out of date and the dragons had evolved in a way the order hadn't anticipated. Thinking about less serious topics such as that kept Marius from losing his mind. His fear for Tahlia was the air he breathed, choking him to near senselessness.

She is strong, Ragewing said.

There is no solution. Ophelia was clear about that. As was Trevain.

As though Marius had summoned him with his silent words to Ragewing, the ghost appeared over Tahlia's inert body. His golden glow illuminated the hollows of her cheeks. She already appeared thinner.

Marius sat Fara on a fallen tree and tucked the cloak tightly around her.

"Can he help her?" Fara asked, her voice raw and rough.

Marius looked in the direction she gazed. She meant Trevain. "I don't know. I'll talk to him."

"Tahlia really likes him. Be nice."

"I've been nice. I just don't trust him because he has no reason to be helping us. Also, I thought he would be trapped in the Kingdom of Spirits. I wonder why he is here and how he managed it."

"Have you ever noticed how much his eyes look like hers?" Fara asked, tilting her head.

Marius left Fara and knelt near Tahlia. Trevain floated beside him. He did have a similar set to his eyes.

"Trevain, can you help her? You know what happened, don't you?"

"I do. I will do what I can to keep her in the realm of the living. I will push her spirit, nudge her, so to speak, with my soul."

"Why?"

"She is my descendant."

Marius's mouth fell open. "Did you always know?"

Trevain shook his head, his horns glittering slightly within their own ghostly light. "I had begun to guess, but... I returned to the realm between worlds and saw the truth there. Mother Twilight guided me. Her mother came from my line."

So that was why Mother Twilight had met with them. Tahlia was one of her own.

"Before you knew that," Marius said, "you were helping us because..."

"Because you aren't evil. The varjuline are. Katk is. It had been ages since I'd seen anyone not of evil spirit in our lands. Aside from a few others like me, of course. Also, I was dreadfully bored."

Marius huffed, tilted his head, and nodded. "Well, I'll take any help you can give. I don't see how my dragon will manage to get us back to the order's castle before Katk arrives there and kills them all."

Trevain leaned close to Tahlia's face, his gaze touching her forehead, her throat. He pressed his hand to his chest and then to Tahlia's. Light blinked brightly around his ghostly fingertips. "Oh, you won't be alone. The goddess's belt has called Tahlia's own to her. Look now," he said, still eyeing Tahlia.

Marius turned to see a thunder of dragons cresting the next peak, their wings dark slashes against the lightening sky.

CHAPTER 30
MARIUS

He stood so quickly that his head spun.

The order was here.

His chest tightened, then relaxed, and he let out a sigh. Mother Twilight's weaving had somehow called the other riders.

"Tahlia already sees the other riders as her family," Trevain said from where he hovered above Tahlia. "Like Fara and her dragon. And you, of course."

Marius stared while Fara hurried to Tahlia's side. Tears silvered her purple cheeks as she took Tahlia's hand. Trevain bobbed in the air beside Fara while she plucked small yellow flowers and mashed them in her palm. Did Fara have Healer training?

Ragewing lifted his head as the order landed one by one, only some of them fitting into the clearing while the rest maneuvered into the edges of the pines that ringed the area.

"What is happening, High Captain?" Titus was the first to speak, leaping from his dragon to salute Marius.

Marius studied the faces of his fellow knights. All of them had come. Every last one, save Ophelia.

Titus's mouth was drawn tight and his eyes narrowed as he took in the scene. "We all experienced the same vision." He truly cared for Tahlia; that much was obvious from the way he kept glancing at her. The two had begun acting like siblings in training and off hours, teasing and checking on one another. Marius approved of the growing bond between them. "We saw Lady Tahlia giving her life for yours when that monster lunged for you."

"It felt like a summons," Maiwenn said.

"But who called you?" Marius asked.

"I did." Tahlia's voice rang out clear behind Marius.

His heart drummed out of rhythm, and he spun. She smiled at him, supporting herself on her elbows. Warmth flooded his veins. Though she looked like a ghost of herself, she was still herself—achingly beautiful. His lovely, brave, soon-to-be mate. Hope flickered brightly in his chest. She was still sick and cursed, but maybe she could heal from this. Maybe between Trevain's help and whatever magic Mother Twilight had awoken in Tahlia , she would be saved.

"Lady Fara gave me some flowers and I feel somewhat better." Tahlia smiled at her squire.

"The curse still threatens her life," Fara said. "I can't stop that. But the *soleils guérisseurs* should slow the decline and give her more time. Albus taught me about the plant."

The other knights simply stared. There was much to explain about what had passed.

Tahlia beamed. "I'm sorry I didn't pay more attention to your interest in healing, Fara. Lady Fara," she said, correcting herself and glancing at Marius.

Marius couldn't fight the broad smile stretching his lips. He couldn't help but hope... "Thank you, Lady Fara."

Marius longed to sprint to Tahlia's side, lift her into his arms, and hide her away from the world. Just for a little while, he wanted her all to himself. To tend her wounds. To learn every bend and curve of her body. To make her laugh, gasp, moan, and sigh. He longed to see her bloom beneath his hands and in his care. She was still terribly pale and hollow-cheeked, but she was awake. Alive. For how long, well, he refused to dwell on that question at the moment.

Keeping a distance from Trevain, the knights swarmed Tahlia.

"Please help me to Lija," Tahlia said to Fara.

Titus put an arm under Tahlia's and hefted her up. Fara took up Tahlia's other arm. They walked the few steps to Lija, then Tahlia settled on the ground and set her cheek against Lija's folded wing, the uninjured one. Titus put a palm on Tahlia's head briefly, and she looked up at him and gave him a mischievous grin. He gently bumped the underside of her chin with a knuckle.

Tahlia coughed and took a shuddering breath as she gathered herself, Titus stepping back so Fara could fuss over her.

"I called you with this woven magic artifact from a goddess in the Kingdom of Spirits," Tahlia said.

Most of the knights blinked in surprise.

Light cut across Enora's freckled face as she took a

poultice from her bag and held it to Fara. "A goddess gave you a gift?"

Fara took the proffered poultice, studied the bottle, then worked on Lija. The dragon grunted in pain but only glared at Fara—no fire involved.

Ewan took a water skin from his bag and handed it to Tahlia. "What happened to Lija?"

"The monster you saw, it was Katk. He carries a plague too," Tahlia said.

Morvan's jet-black eyes studied Tahlia. "And you're injured? I'm so confused. Somebody explain everything, please."

"Stay back, just in case," Tahlia said, waving a shaky hand and nearly touching Claudia's whipping orange tail.

"I don't think the curse will touch them," Trevain said from behind the group.

The knights glanced his way, their faces drawn with wary awe.

Atticus shoved his hair back between his silver horns and turned to face Tahlia. "The curse? What curse?"

Lija was trying to partially cocoon Tahlia. Titus helped by moving a middling-sized boulder out of the way. Marius flexed his hands, wishing he was the one to physically help Tahlia. But he wasn't sure if his touch would worsen her condition. Plus, he wasn't sure he could control himself if he had his hands on Tahlia just now. He'd been so lost, so desperate, when she'd given herself for his life. If he touched her again—when he touched her—it would be to claim her in full as his mate and his ultimate joy. There wouldn't be time for explanations about Katk or Mother Twilight.

"What exactly happened?" Titus asked.

Then Tahlia and Marius told them everything about this unplanned mission in detail. More questions flowed from the knights. Tahlia answered, the tentative happiness in her tired eyes lighting a flicker of hope in Marius's heart.

Trevain also explained the history of his kingdom.

"And as much as I hate to say it," Tahlia said in a slightly broken voice, interrupting him when he began regaling everyone with the architectural details of the ruins the varjuline had inhabited, "I truly believe Ophelia cast this curse."

Maiwenn grunted and chewed the inside of her cheek. "So our new commander woke this plague monster who is set on killing all those with Mistgold blood?"

Her tone wasn't harsh, only curious, as if she was confirming what she'd been told. Something in the way they'd been called by Mother Twilight's belt at Tahlia's waist had changed the way she looked at Tahlia. Somehow Maiwenn and the rest knew of Tahlia's sacrifice.

"Did something change between us? I mean, I'm glad but..." Tahlia waited for Maiwenn to answer.

"We all felt your sacrifice. Whatever you did," Maiwenn said, her gaze flicking from Marius to Tahlia, "I'm not sure what happened, but we definitely felt it."

"The sacrifice and the Call of the Weaver," Trevain

said. "Our goddess, Mother Twilight, gave Lady Tahlia a belt of our people's magic. She woke its power by giving all to another. The weaving sent a beacon to those she trusts with her life."

Atticus and Claudia exchanged a sheepish grin, then looked to Tahlia with respect shining in their eyes. Maiwenn nodded at Tahlia, crossing her arms and smiling. Titus knocked his head gently against the side of Tahlia's. He was becoming more dragon than Fae, Marius thought, silently chuckling.

I agree, Ragewing said into Marius's mind.

Marius laughed out loud then. *I'll have to tell him so.*

Tahlia reached for Fara, who helped her up. "I think I can ride. Can we move now?

Fara clucked like an old hen. "You shouldn't be going anywhere. You look like death."

"Katk isn't going to wait and I refuse to be left here."

Titus nodded at Tahlia, then eyed Marius. Marius gave a nod.

"We ride now," Marius said. "Lady Tahlia, you will be tied to Titus's saddle. He will hold you fast. I trust him." He looked to Fara. "Squire, you'll be with me. Ragewing will carry Lija for the first leg, and then, Sir Atticus and Revel, you will carry her the next." Atticus's Heartsworn was nearly as large as Ragewing.

"Aye, High Captain," Tahlia said, her eyes full of a fevered desperation.

Marius swallowed, wishing there was time to pray to every Old One he'd ever heard of. She was still worried she was going to die. So was he.

"Aye, High Captain," the other knights echoed.

Marius barked more orders, falling into the comfort of routine and familiar activities. He gave Ragewing a healthy serving of dragonbread and made certain Lija had the same treatment.

"Before we take off, if you see any plants with blood-red leaves, pluck them and eat them. Once the leaves are in your stomach, you'll be able to communicate with your dragons through your mind."

Claudia rubbed her orange forehead. "I can't take any more wild revelations."

The rest of the knights had gone silent, their dragons turning their attention to Marius.

"It's true," Tahlia said, her voice sounding weak again. "I can hear Lija in my head."

"Lija?" Brutus pursed his purple lips and fisted his hands, which Marius knew was a sign that the warrior was losing patience and more than ready to take action.

"Her name is Vodolija. Lija is a nickname," Tahlia said.

Then she crumpled to the ground. Marius went cold and hot all at once, his feet moving before he could order himself to keep his distance. He stopped short, Fara's hand suddenly on his chest.

Titus was helping Tahlia up.

"We've got her, High Captain," Fara said.

Gritting his teeth, he nodded. "Let's ride. We are running out of time to try to break this curse."

Everyone mounted—Fara with Marius, Tahlia with Titus—and they were off in moments.

"How do we set things right?" Titus called out in his Mistgold voice.

The wind tore at Marius's knotted hair and blew Fara's scent across his face. She was seated in front of him, murmuring ridiculous phrases to Ragewing.

"And if you don't eat me, I'll steal anything you want from the kitchens. You look like a guy who enjoys chocolate."

Ragewing grunted loudly and increased speed to fly beside Titus and his Spikeback, Ptol.

"We trap Katk with fire and bring him to Ophelia," Marius said to Titus, using his Mistgold voice.

It felt so wrong to address another rider as simply their name. Especially one who had been deemed their commander. But he shoved that urge to be the disciplined knight away. Ophelia didn't deserve a title. She deserved death.

"If the monster touches you, you will eventually be drained of all your life energy," Marius called out. "Keep your distance and only use flame, short spear, and arrow to fight."

Ewan's Spikeback, Angus, flew just behind Titus and Ptol. Ewan had a short spear and three more tucked under his leg for easy reach. Atticus, Enora, and Ewan would have their bows at the ready.

"To your units!" Marius called.

The knights and their dragons joined their units and flew in the standard pointed formation for a long flight when speed was paramount.

If you see anything you believe is a sign of Katk, please tell me. Nothing is too small, Marius said silently to Ragewing.

How about we check that valley to the south? If I were a

lumbering giant, I'd choose the lowlands over these spiking mountains.

Let's give it a go. Marius held up a hand and directed the order toward said valley.

Ragewing led the three units over a pale limestone outcropping. Farms ripe with spring plantings of onions, cabbages, and the first shoots of root vegetables spread below like a painting of a peaceful life Marius would never know. Not that he longed to be a farmer, but the idea of working alongside others without the interruption of dark magic was certainly a draw.

"She'll be all right," Fara said, twisting to speak to him over her shoulder.

"I don't know. I..."

"Ah. You still can't speak of the curse and what you know."

"No."

Fara's hair fluttered in the wind as she looked toward Titus. Tahlia was lashed to him and Ptol's saddle. It would be difficult for Titus to fire arrows in his position. Once Ptol was out of fire, Titus would need to fall back. Perhaps serving as a distraction, out of reach of Katk, but still helpful. Marius tucked that strategy away for later use.

As if looking her way had shaken her awake, Tahlia opened her eyes.

Marius took a deep breath.

"If you scowl at her like that, she's going to pass out again," Fara said.

"If my glares affected her in any way, she'd have given up on me the first day we met."

Fara laughed. "Still. Smile at your lady, High Captain. She probably needs some reassurance. It can't be fun shaking hands with Death every hour or so."

A shudder raked through Marius. "I'd rather you not joke about her condition."

"It's that or scream and cry. You pick."

"Fine. Jokes, it is."

There! Ragewing veered in a southwest direction, taking the units with him.

Katk stormed through a boggy area, dark water splashing up around his knees and gnarled trees breaking like tall grass around him.

Good spot, friend.

Marius gave orders for the units to surround him. "Once he is contained, we escort him as quickly as possible back to the castle."

"High Captain!" Titus waved a hand.

Tahlia was awake, upright, and her mouth was moving, but the wind and Katk's roars tried to cloak her words.

Titus took over for her and shouted, "She's saying there's no way our dragons' fire will last long enough to return to Dragon Tail, to the castle! She wants us to fly back and grab Ophelia."

"Absolutely not," Marius said. "You're sick, Lady Tahlia." A thought haunted him, far more frightening than any ghost or shadowling—she was not merely ill. She was dying. "Not possible!"

"I will murder you if you let her do this," Fara said, a promise in her voice that worried Marius even though she was but a squire.

"I wouldn't blame you," he said.

Then there was no more time for discussion because they were within Katk's extended reach. The dragons encircled Katk.

This had to work or all of them were dead and the order would be no more.

"Unit one blast!" Marius called out.

CHAPTER 31
MARIUS

Marius had Ragewing fall back to protect their cargo—Lija, who was roaring in frustration. Fire spilled from the rest of the unit one dragons: blue, orange, purple, and gold. Katk shrieked and batted at the riders and their mounts. The monster's forefinger clipped Titus's Spikeback. Ptol spun and his riders jerked harshly upward, Titus dropping his bow and grasping Tahlia, whose eyes were wide open.

Marius's heart thudded at the back of his throat. With every fiber of his being, he longed to be the one protecting his intended mate.

Katk surged toward them as Ptol tried to right himself.

"Unit two!" Marius ordered. "Don't expend all your fire though. Watch your levels!" They had to reserve enough to prod this monster toward home. Such a mad plan!

Taking turns, including unit three as well, they had Katk panting and lumbering in the right direction after another hour of fitful fighting. The journey would be arduous, to say the least.

"I have an idea!" Tahlia called out. She sounded stronger and her color had mostly returned. Gods, this curse was taunting them, fading and returning over and over again.

Marius could hardly hear her above the noise of fire and monster and wind.

Her energy is stronger. Her body is fighting the curse, Ragewing said. *The blooms that Lady Fara administered have helped indeed.*

Marius whispered a prayer of gratitude. *I didn't realize you could sense the energy and health of another being.*

There is much Fae do not know about dragons.

I look forward to learning from you. If you choose to share.

A deep chuckle rumbled through Marius's mind. *Some things, I will share. Some are not for Fae to know.*

I won't be like my ancestors, harsh and cruel to those around them. If you decide on secrecy, I will honor that.

And that's another reason you're my rider.

Katk groaned and stalked through the countryside, his movements prodded by the dragons' flames. He whirled and swatted at Maiwenn and her Seabreak, Donan. Katk's fist hit Donan's side, and the dragon screeched. Lija shrieked with him. Maiwenn's eyes went wide. She dropped from the saddle and fell toward the ground.

Donan let out a spine-rattling sound of agony and dove for his rider.

Go! Marius called to Ragewing, who immediately plunged.

A jagged line of boulders marked the ground below Maiwenn. Claudia and Justus shouted her name.

Marius held his breath. They weren't going to make it. Maiwenn was going to die.

Ragewing angled to swoop below Maiwenn, and Donan dove straight for her.

Katk shouted as if in triumph, and rage poured from Marius's very pores. He pressed his palm against Ragewing's shoulder. *Please. Faster.*

I'm trying, rider!

Donan roared, the sound splintering the air. Katk broke free of the dragon fire and lunged at Ptol and Titus.

Marius's entire life was being ripped to pieces, like a crumbling piece of parchment left in the sun and wind too long. He needed his knights. All of them. They were the only ones he trusted to help Tahlia, to help him if she couldn't be saved.

The rocks flew toward them and Maiwenn was tumbling like a corn husk doll, her limbs taunted by the wind.

Donan stretched out his long neck and snatched Maiwenn from the air. But they were going to hit the ground and Maiwenn wouldn't be able to handle the crash.

Under them!

Ragewing veered harshly and came up just under Donan's tipped wing. Ragewing bumped the other dragon, the rocks so, so close. With the aid of Ragewing's bump, Donan rose sharply into the sky with Maiwenn secured between his teeth as dragons did with the very young of their kind.

Ragewing followed Donan, and Marius shouted orders, "All units, stop Katk! Turn him around!"

A sheep farm appeared beyond a crevice in the lowlands. The giant was heading that way, of that Marius had no doubt. Either with the golden plague or with simple fists and feet, Katk would kill everything in sight. These folks in the foothills of the Shrouded Mountains had Mistgold blood just as he did. And he had sworn an oath to protect them.

"Three! Unit three, take the lead!" His voice boomed off a bank of clouds shifting between Ragewing and Ewan on Angus's spiked form.

Ewan raised a fist to indicate he'd heard and would do as ordered. His dark, bald head reflected the scant sunlight as Angus dove toward the giant. Brutus on his Spikeback followed close behind, flanked by Cyrus and Lucius on their Heartsworns. Their fire rippled across Katk's face and the monster dropped back, his foot crushing a bridge spanning a broad and spring-muddied river.

"Unit two! Back them up! Southward until we hit the pit, then we push him northwest!" Marius ordered. "Unit three, fall back! We will fill in there!"

He waved to his unit behind him and they circled unit three, flaring fire as unit three filtered in between unit one, flying between them in expert-level formation. He was proud of these riders. And crushed that Tahlia wasn't among them.

A dark shape burst through the scattered clouds and every thought shattered.

Ophelia. Her cheeks and chin glistened as if she had been... No, she couldn't have been weeping. Ophelia didn't cry, not even once since he'd known her. And they had seen a great deal. Including her father's death.

Had she truly killed him? Was this all her doing?

Tahlia believed that. Marius didn't want to believe it, but Ophelia had never been a good person. She'd followed orders. Well, except concerning those damned gloves of hers. She must have felt so terribly desperate to be cruel to her dragon.

He couldn't even imagine what he was thinking when he had thought to be her mate, to wed her and have younglings with her. He'd been an idiot. A fool. Ophelia was even worse than he realized. Not just cruel to a creature because of desperation. But cruel in general. She, like Katk, was a monster.

Ophelia lifted her hand, and black and gold magic spun from her fingertips like she was casting a net.

The world's edges fogged.

Marius couldn't seem to recall what he and the others were doing here, up in the air, above the creature designed to enact proper revenge.

CHAPTER 32
TAHLIA

Tahlia felt hollowed out, weak, and unsubstantial. Her strength came and went in unpredictable waves. Focusing on the battle wasn't easy as her vision blurred off and on. She was a cracked remnant of something that was once strong on the back of a dragon that wasn't hers.

But she wasn't quite useless yet. Not during her now-and-again alert periods.

Wasn't it just lovely that Ophelia showed up as her eyes opened again?

Tahlia worked the knot holding her in place against Titus.

"What are you doing?" Titus shifted his weight and she felt his breath on her head.

"I don't need this."

"The hells you don't."

She finished untying herself from him and the saddle, coiled the rope, and quickly tucked it into one of the saddlebags while Titus swore.

"The High Captain will murder me if I live through this," Titus grumbled.

"Fly over her dragon." Tahlia tried not to dwell on the fact that Lija hadn't spoken into her mind in a long while.

Titus held her tighter. "What? No."

"Yes. She isn't bonded to that Terror, so I plan to kick her arse right off the dragon's back. Let's see if that ends Marius's curse and puts that monster down. It can't hurt."

"She's our new commander."

"And she's a murderer who raises demonic monsters," Tahlia said.

"You don't know that for sure."

"If you're going to say it, at least pretend to believe it, Titus. I saw that magic. The stuff she just flung at Katk." Ophelia had thrown power at Katk, right? Or had it been aimed at Marius? "Does Marius look normal? I can't quite see what he's up to with these half-human eyes."

"He fights Katk still. Well, Ragewing isn't firing, but I think he's just pulling us back."

"Did he give that order before I woke up again?"

"No, but he is falling back." Titus let out a whistle and Ptol tipped his wings and flapped them hard. They shifted away from Katk. "And just because the Terror isn't bonded to her doesn't mean it won't whip around and gulp you down as a journey snack."

"Nah, he won't hurt me. It'll all happen too fast."

"Says the female who is currently dancing very close with Death himself."

"Hey, don't count me out yet."

Maiwenn shouted, her voice strained and reedy. Tahlia and Titus turned to see her pointing at Marius and Ragewing.

The dark magic that Ophelia wielded, which Marius also had since she'd cursed him, engulfed Ragewing's head. The dragon shook himself hard, Marius holding tight with his legs and his body tense. Marius's eyes were wide and unblinking.

"The High Captain isn't himself!" Titus called out.

Tahlia felt like she was falling. Fara still clung to him. And Lija was clutched in Ragewing's talons. "Marius! Please!"

Ragewing twisted in the air, then faced Ptol and opened his great maw.

"He's firing on us!" Tahlia gripped the edge of the saddle, knowing what was coming next.

Ptol dove.

Heat seared the air just above Tahlia's head. Cursing Ophelia's name, Tahlia touched her hair to make sure it was still there.

"I can't fight him," Titus said, steering Ptol around to come up between Justus, Claudia, and their dragons.

Ophelia laughed, a short quick sound. "What's wrong, human? Are things not exactly going your way? Attack them!" she ordered, sweeping all three units with her vicious gaze.

Her Green-flanked Terror let out an ear-cracking roar that Katk mimicked.

Ragewing angled around to aim at Ptol once more.

Katk reached for units two and three, and Ewan, Cyrus, and Enora were nearly swiped out of the air. Their dragons roared with flame, but their fire was almost spent.

Ragewing hovered in front of Ptol. Marius tapped his shoulder, and the bespelled Heartsworn opened his talons. Lija dropped into the open sky. Fara shrieked at the same time as Tahlia, whose heartbeat whirred in a deafening pitch. Then Marius shoved Fara off Ragewing.

Lija fell in a disjointed pattern as she tried to use her broken wing. Her roars and Fara's screams ripped Tahlia in two.

Trevain materialized beside her. With a grim look, he reached out a palm and shut her eyes.

Tahlia saw Mother Twilight.

The goddess smiled, her face wrinkling beautifully. She and Tahlia sat side by side in the goddess' flowered forest meadow with butterflies dancing about and tree seeds drifting through the warm air. Peace filled Tahlia as she helped Mother Twilight feed finely spun lavender wool onto a spool.

"What do you want of this life, Weaver?" the goddess asked.

"To live it in full."

"Ah, but do you? Grief is a part of living in full."

A stone formed in Tahlia's belly and she took a slow breath. "I've experienced grief."

"Yes. You're not a... Was it a *marshmallow* you told your fated mate about?" A smile stretched her ancient lips.

Surprise shrank the stone inside Tahlia's stomach. Her limbs stopped shaking and strength flowed through her hands and legs again. She laughed. "Yes. I've been through terrible challenges."

"But you must do so again. And again. It is the way of things." The goddess lifted her free hand as if to indicate the world at large.

Tahlia's belly tightened around the stone. "But perhaps not yet?" She smiled and looked into Mother Twilight's deep-set eyes.

The butterflies stilled in the air, the wood thrushes and insects halted their song, and the tree seeds hung like unspoken thoughts in the sunny space around them.

The goddess nodded at the wool in Tahlia's hands. The lavender strands flared with purple light. "You have the power to do as you see fit."

Tahlia inhaled the sweet scent of the meadow. "I do?"

Mother Twilight pursed her lips and narrowed her eyes. "Well, mostly."

"How can I save them all?"

"Hmm. Recall your first wild idea. It's you who sees the patterns you may use as you see fit. Trust in yourself. But remember, you must feel every emotion during the varied seasons of life. Pain and triumph, joy and loss, regret and anticipation. They are connected, too."

She lifted a hand, and sparkling threads of lavender, ruby red, black, and blue appeared in a flash of light. The strands of colors linked the butterflies, the tall grasses, and the branches of the highest trees, and they were tied also to Tahlia's fingers and the pulse points at her throat...

"You see them now, Weaver?"

Tahlia nodded, marveling at the threads linking Mother Twilight to her as well. They were as black as midnight, lovely and strong. "I do."

Opening her eyes, Tahlia braced for the shock of leaving the goddess' peaceful presence and heading back into battle. She ordered Titus, "Fly over Ophelia. Now."

Titus didn't hesitate this time; he pulled in a quick breath that moved them both, then urged Ptol to shoot for the Green-flanked Terror. Fire touched Tahlia's elbow and knee. Titus called out in pain but kept his seat. Ptol snarled and hovered above the Terror.

Threads of life connected every life here. The ground, the sky, the animals, the dragons, the Fae...

Tahlia leapt from Ptol's back, a jet of flame searing her back as she landed on the Terror. Ophelia was up and throwing a dagger before Tahlia caught her balance. But the threads were there, and they spoke some silent language that said where to set foot, hand, and will.

Slipping her head to the right, Tahlia dodged the flying blade. Ophelia ran along the Terror's spine, nearly falling as she reached Tahlia, but reach her she did. Ophelia slammed a fist toward Tahlia's chin. Tahlia threw up an arm and knocked the strike to the side before cracking Ophelia's ribs with a thrust of her palm. Ophelia dropped back, holding her side and heaving. Her blue-green hair fluttered around her face.

Tahlia bared her fangs. "You poisoned me, didn't you?"

"Of course I did, fool." Ophelia launched herself forward.

Crouching, Tahlia gripped one of the Terror's spikes

as the dragon listed to one side. Ophelia fell to her stomach and grabbed onto another spike, the Terror's wing nearly battering her in the process.

Tahlia stood as the threads showed the Terror was about to even out his flight. Confusion swarmed his mind, or at least that was what the threads suggested. Maybe he would circle and hover and await an attack from one of the others to do more than that. But one thing was abundantly clear...

"Your dragon is trying to get rid of you," she said to Ophelia.

"Ha! As if you know anything about dragons, human."

The dragon dipped, and they flew up for a second, both females scrambling for a hold on the creature. If she'd not been weakened by the cursed plague, she'd have had no problem, not with the threads' help. But her body trembled with fatigue again, and she couldn't get her lungs to fill with air. The Terror leveled himself once more, flying higher, the fight between possessed Marius and his likewise controlled Ragewing and the other members of the order below them. Thank the Old Ones that the other riders and dragons were able to keep Ragewing from firing on them by peppering him and Marius with attacks. Marius had his bow out though and Tahlia fought to focus on the fight going on in front of her positionally. Even though she saw the threads clearly, her heart demanded that she check on Marius and everyone else.

Forcing herself to turn back to Ophelia, Tahlia studied the female's red-tinged eyes and how her lips were pulled back into a grimace. Ophelia was just a sad, sad person.

"I can't believe you murdered your father." Anger made Tahlia's skin itch. "Why did you do it?"

"I sacrificed everything for this order and Marius." Spittle flew from Ophelia's mouth as she made it to her feet and started toward Tahlia. "You wouldn't understand that kind of selflessness, human."

Tahlia lifted her sleeve to show the golden boils that had erupted when she'd grabbed Marius. "Wouldn't I?"

Ophelia's eyes went wide. "The ritual worked." She flung a hand in Katk's general direction, but Tahlia didn't glance away. The threads told her what she needed to know. "The monster did that to you?"

"Marius's curse did this to me when I pushed him back to save his life."

A sick grin crawled across Ophelia's lips. "It all worked. The demon, the ritual..."

"Whatever you did woke up this monster and he is determined to kill everyone with Mistgold blood. How do you see that as success?" For a moment, black spots dotted Tahlia's vision.

Ophelia laughed loudly and shot forward. Threads, black and blue, wound through the air, connecting dragon scales, wings, Ophelia, Tahlia, and the twist of wind that buffeted them. The sparkling lines showed Tahlia exactly what to do and when to do it.

Shaking slightly, Tahlia simply lifted a foot and launched the witch off the dragon.

Bellowing, Katk caught Ophelia. Golden boils erupted over her face, and she screamed. Her shrieking faded to nothing and she disappeared inside the monster's fist. He stumbled, on the verge of falling.

Katk's creator had formed him to destroy those Fae with Mistgold blood and not even the fact that Ophelia was his champion could save her. In fact, it was that very fact that had doomed her from the first time she'd done whatever ritual it took to raise him. Katk had met his champion at last, only to kill her, and with that move, end himself as well.

Tahlia winced at the tragic waste of Commander Gaius's life and Ophelia's riding talent. Dropping to her knees, Tahlia trembled as the remainder of her strength left her body. Her skin was on fire, the dragon fire burns battling to outdo the pain of the golden boils. The sounds of the fight jumbled in her ears as if she was underwater.

Rider, don't give up. It was Lija, her voice reedy and frail.

I won't. I can see it...

Atticus and Ewan shouted for Tahlia. She turned their way as she crawled to the Terror's saddle. Beside them, Maiwenn waved her arms. Her Seabreak, Donan, clasped both Lija and Fara in his talons. Trevain floated nearby and a host of spirits the same golden shade had joined him.

Every ounce of air left Tahlia's lungs. They were alive. She'd seen it in the threads, but it was impossible not to fear the worst anyway.

Then her heart drew her eyes to Marius.

Ragewing flew toward Katk, who had gone to his knees on the earth below.

Were Marius and Ragewing still held by the curse's power? Where was Ophelia?

Tahlia searched the threads and found nothing.

Had Ophelia portalled somewhere or disappeared using more dark magic?

Ragewing blazed the back of Katk's head, and even though the Heartsworn's fire was as tattered as an old cloak, hope lit a flame of its own inside Tahlia. They were fighting Katk and, hopefully, Ophelia and the curse, too.

Katk's massive body pounded to the earth. Boulders lifted from their resting spots to roll down the foothills in an avalanche. The debris cut its way messily down the land. Trees snapped like twigs and fell. In the distance, mountain goats bleated in alarm and scattered.

The ground around the giant vibrated harshly, sending more trees and rocks into the air and tumbling.

"What in the..." Titus hissed.

Black earth churned and crawled over Katk's form. A scream erupted from Katk's clasped fist. His fingers fell open to show Ophelia, limp and unmoving. The dirt smothered them both—monster and champion—and silence bloomed.

Tahlia fell forward onto the Terror. "Thanks for not killing me, pal." She patted the deep green of the dragon's scales once and darkness poured over her senses.

CHAPTER 33
MARIUS

Marius's mind cleared abruptly.

Rider, we were under the suggestion of dark magic.

I know, well, at least I know it now.

Ophelia is dead. The curse is broken. I don't feel its power around us at all now.

Thank the gods.

Ragewing wheeled around, and there was Tahlia sitting like a young one's forgotten doll on the back of the Green-flanked Terror. Marius took a deep breath and tried not to panic that Tahlia was riding another dragon, an unbonded one.

He says he will carry her home. Lija is in too much pain to argue, but I feel as if she would approve. Anything to help her rider. The Terror calls Lady Tahlia the Weaver.

You are speaking to him?

Yes, but he speaks even less than most of us dragons. He has been betrayed in the past and is closed off to any bonds.

Because of Ophelia?

That, and I think another instance earlier on in his life. He will not share more than the vague idea of that history.

Well, he won't need to carry her for long.

"We land at the lower pass!" he called out with his Mistgold voice.

The grassy dip in the mountains appeared shortly thereafter and everyone landed. Marius hurried to the Terror, hands outstretched toward the large green dragon and his head bowed in submission.

"Thank you for carrying my mate," he said quietly.

The Terror regarded him cooly but lowered his wing and shoulder so Marius could climb up and retrieve Tahlia. She was completely out—eyelids shuttered and body limp. Her chest moved in slow and stuttering breaths as if pain tried to smother her. He swallowed and carried her quickly to the spot where everyone tended to wounds. Bottles of unguents, vials of potion, and tiny bags of healing herbs littered the clover-covered ground.

Limping, Fara walked to where Marius laid Tahlia on the green growth.

"What can we do for her? Let her sleep or try to wake her with herbs?" Marius asked Fara.

"She should sleep. Her body is most likely trying to heal from the internal damage the plague wrought on her organs. I can't believe she jumped from one dragon to another. I can't believe she fought Ophelia and won."

Pride rose in Marius's chest, the joy warring with the chill of fear in his heart. "She's a wonder, my Lady of the Skies."

Fara smiled, then winced, holding her left arm tenderly.

He nodded toward her arm. "Is it broken?"

"I think so."

"Want me to help you splint it for the rest of the journey?"

"Please."

Marius did so, using a few branches he broke from a nearby beech. He then went to Lija and oversaw Maiwenn and Atticus as they applied healing unguent to the Seabreak's wing. Marius splinted the two broken places along the top of her wing.

"The lower break will have to heal as best it can. The bones are too shattered to be splinted," he said, glancing at Atticus.

Atticus nodded in agreement, and Maiwenn opened her mouth as if to say something, but she remained quiet.

Marius knew what she had been about to say. Lija might never fly again.

Swallowing that worry down, he ordered Enora and her Heartsworn to carry Lija *en talon* as it was called when one dragon toted another with careful talons.

Once the other riders were ready, Titus helped Marius situate Tahlia on his lap on Ragewing's back. As they lifted off, the units arranging themselves in the sky, Marius tucked a lock of black hair behind Tahlia's ear.

"Soon, I'll see those honey-gold eyes of yours again. I know it."

She didn't move a muscle and so he began to repeat the same phrase in his mind over and over like a chant, like one of the Druid's spells, in hopes that it was the truth.

She is too alive to die. She is too alive to die. She is too alive to die.

Ragewing remained quiet as they flew, and the journey home was ages long.

If they had broken the curse, and the plague was gone, why was Tahlia still unconscious? Had her body suffered too much damage already? It was inaccurate to blame himself, but guilt whipped his soul regardless.

The riders soared up the crest of Dragon Tail Peak. Wind pushed at their backs, chilly but scented with the first of the summer flowers. Marius and Ragewing led all three units over the two sets of walls surrounding the order's keep. They landed in the arena, and Remus was there to greet them.

Marius climbed down Ragewing's shoulder, and Remus helped him get Tahlia down. Titus hurried to help as well.

"What's the status here?" Marius asked Remus as he lifted Tahlia into his arms once more. "Speak freely around Sir Titus."

Remus inclined his head in a shallow bow. "The Bloodworkers are meeting now. As per the order rules, the Bloodworkers took charge the moment the majority of the knights went rogue. They are deciding whether or not to send word to the king about potentially disbanding the entire order so they may start anew."

"Exactly how do they propose to kick us out when we are bonded to dragons?"

"There are whispers that Bloodworker Cavalon has knowledge of a potion that would break those bonds and allow the dragons to choose new riders."

Ragewing growled in Marius's mind.

"How do they suppose they will talk the dragons into taking such a potion?"

Remus shrugged, then ran a hand down Ragewing's leg, eyeing the dragon's dirtied talons and a smear of char along his scales. Marius didn't know which dragon had fired on them while they were controlled by Ophelia, but it didn't matter. The fight had been madness. There was no blame to set anywhere besides on the shade of Ophelia.

Gaius, I'm sorry I wasn't there, at your back, to prevent this tragedy.

The wind lifted the ends of his tangled hair and stirred Tahlia's wavy locks too. He wanted to believe it was the spirit of the old commander, giving them his blessing.

"Sir Titus, send for the Healers that we can trust. As soon as you and Ptol are ready, fly to the king and queen. Tell them what has happened here, of Ophelia's dark magic, the monster, and my curse. Inform them of what Remus has told us. Cavalon is no friend to the king."

Titus nodded and hurried away.

Marius met Healer Albus at the side door to the riders' wing in the keep.

"Tell me everything," Albus said, waving Marius into the keep.

She is too alive to die. Wake up, Tahlia. Please, wake up.

CHAPTER 34
TAHLIA

Wool and thorns cocooned Tahlia. Her lips wouldn't part because her tongue was so dry that it stuck fast to the roof of her mouth. Her eyes refused to open even a crack. She heard the rumble and lilt of male and female voices, but the thorny wool enclosed her head and ears, too. She couldn't make out any words. She longed to shout for them to take this off of her, to pull her free...

Dreams and nightmares twisted through her mind. She fell through the clouds. Lija shrieked. Fara called her name. Marius ordered someone to stand down, to back away. None of it made any sense. Her mind swam and her stomach rolled. A bitter taste hit her tongue.

Her eyes flew open. Threads of connection flickered here and there, but they were faint, like ghosts of what she'd seen during the fight with Ophelia.

Fara was there, mouth dropping open. "You're not dead! Woooo!"

Tahlia gave a weak laugh. "What's happening?"

Light stone walls surrounded her. A long window let in the soft glow of maybe sunset?

"You're home. I mean, at the order's keep."

"Is Marius... Lija?"

Fara held out her hands. "They're both fine." Her features had gone flat, her usual fire dimmed for some purpose—perhaps to calm Tahlia.

"You're not telling me something."

Taking a breath, Fara gripped Tahlia's fingers lightly. "Healer Albus is worried that Lija will, um, take a long time to fly again."

Tahlia squeezed Fara's hand. "But she will fly again?"

"He's not sure. Now, be still. I need to mix up a draught for you." Fara went to the long table at the far side of the room and banged about with a mortar and pestle. She whistled as she worked.

Tahlia closed her eyes and took a deep breath, trying to slow her heart.

Lija?

Ah, rider. You're awake.

It's so good to hear your voice. Understatement of this eon. Tahlia didn't want to bring up the flying issue. *Can you sense my Weaver magic?*

Yes, but it rests. You don't need it at the moment. I believe it will rise if you call to it.

I have no idea how to do that.

I assume whatever you choose to do to call that power forth will work, as you are its master.

Thanks, Lija. I'm just so happy you're all right.

I am angry but alive and grateful, too. But I to go into

battle with you properly. Don't say that won't happen someday.

I don't think that will be a problem.

Fara returned with a tiny crockery cup and held it out for Tahlia to take. "So glad you're not dead."

Tahlia finished the cup and set it on the side table. Fara gulped a sob and lunged, landing a hug on Tahlia that could have beat every hug in history.

They cried together, laughing too, and trading words that made little sense to the world but everything to them.

A soft knock sounded at the open doorway. Fara moved away and there was Marius. A shuddering sigh left Tahlia. He was whole. His eyes were his eyes. The curse was gone. She could leap from one mountain to another. Nothing was impossible if she had Fara, Lija, and Marius.

"I can come back later if you would like more time to catch up," he said, his deep voice a warm blanket, a sparkling fire, the best wine in all the realms.

"Oh, no," Fara said, gathering her bag and a cloak she'd had draped over her chair. "I wouldn't come between you two for anything." She pointed a finger at Marius and scowled. "But you'd better not get her all riled up. She needs rest."

Marius's stormy eyes twinkled. "I wouldn't dare."

Tahlia truly hoped he would.

Fara waved a goodbye and scurried out, mumbling something about the kitchens and some fresh bread.

Striding forward on his long, long legs, Marius gave

Tahlia what could only be described as a dark smile. She loved every bit of it.

"You gave me a terrible scare, little salty."

He sat on the side of the bed and she turned to her side to face him.

"I was only getting you back for all that creepy possessed stuff you threw at me."

Wincing, he reached for her arm. His warm fingers curled around her cool skin, and she swallowed. "I'm so sorry, Tahlia. Truly. I should have been far more aggressive with outing Ophelia as the villain she was."

"Yes, you should have. But I should have spoken up and demanded to be heard, too." She traced a line across his knuckles and the scars he'd gained from fighting over the years. She wanted to learn about them all. "But she's gone for good. Right?"

"She is." He leaned forward and tucked her hair behind her ear. The graze of his thumb on her cheek threw sparks down her neck.

Leaning into his hand, she breathed him in and let a tear fall down her cheek. He cupped her face in the way he had pretended to back in the forest in the land of spirits.

She savored the moment, reveling in the peace that emanated from him. "It's so good to be able to touch you."

"I confess. I'm still nervous about doing so," Marius said.

"But the curse is broken. All is well."

His jaw worked, and he looked out the window. The

reflection of the clouds flew across his slitted irises. "It is. But it was..."

Tahlia rubbed the back of his hand. "It was awful. Yes. All of it. Except for that wild magic the goddess gave me."

She told him the tale of the threads and the strange vision of Mother Twilight during the fight.

Marius was shaking his head and the hint of a smile pulled the corners of his mouth. "You grow more amazing every day, my love."

She sat up and he quickly moved to help her get comfortable with more pillows than anyone could possibly need at her back. Then she couldn't take it one more second and she wrapped her arms around him in full. More tears burned their way down her cheeks. He buried his face in her hair.

"My lady. I love you so," he whispered, his breath hot on her ear.

He took her face in his hands and kissed her softly but thoroughly, his lips floating across hers and his thumbs stroking the pulse point under her jaw. His tongue darted into her mouth and her heart skipped. She pushed into the kiss, shoving her hands into his Fae-white hair.

"You can't stand that I'm properly groomed, can you?" he asked, chuckling against her temple.

"No, I can't." She laughed. "I'll always be the one to muss you up, High Captain."

"Oh, you'll have to call me commander now, I'm afraid."

She pulled away. "Really? How long have I been out?"

"A few days, but we had to act quickly. A few of the more power-grasping Bloodworkers attempted to press their case and try their hand at leading the order. We had to put a quick stop to that madness."

"How did you manage?"

"Well, it began with Fara attacking the main player in the attempted coup."

Tahlia barked a laugh. "Of course it did."

"Once we pulled her off, I knew we had to act swiftly. Fara was only doing what all of us wished to do. That female knows no fear when it comes to defending you."

"And you now, too, I bet."

"Yes, said Bloodworker made a derogatory remark about our upcoming ceremony. By the way, you need to choose where to hold the ritual. King Lysanael and Queen Revna have invited us to bond at the menhir near the Gwerhune, but they said there is also a sacred standing stone on the land the king gave you upon winning the tournament."

Tahlia held her breath. "What ceremony?"

"You're welcome to call it off, but I assumed you would want to wed me as soon as you were awake."

Tahlia jumped at him, landing in his lap, body aching and heart dancing. She kissed his forehead, nose, cheeks, chin, and down his gorgeous neck. "Yes, yes, yes!"

He laughed loud then, a sound that would have brought her back to life if the curse had won the day. Gods, he was so beautiful. The knot in his throat bobbed as he laughed, and the corners of his eyes crinkled.

"Please always laugh like that, my delicious commander." She slid her palms up his broad chest, enjoying the feel of the powerful muscle under his thin woolen tunic.

He looked down at her, eyes practically smoking. "I will do as you ask, Lady of the Skies. You are an absolute madwoman in battle, and in bed, and I am at your mercy in every situation." He kissed her again. "But don't tell anyone else or I'll lose my job."

They laughed, and it was a dream she hadn't dared to dream coming true. They were healed, happy, and together. She refrained from pinching herself to make certain she was awake, but it was a close thing.

"So when is the bonding ritual? Do we have a date?" she asked, more than prepared to leave the Healers' quarters immediately.

CHAPTER 35
TAHLIA

In the end, they decided to wed on the castle's grounds. It only seemed fitting for two Mist Knights to marry amid dragons and the highest peaks. Tahlia selected a cluster of crystals as the sacred handfasting site. Marius had approved of the creativity and told her that Ragewing was in full agreement. Lija preferred it as well because she still wasn't able to fly, so she couldn't travel far.

The Druid had arrived to see if he could help Lija heal. Fara couldn't stop grinning at the idea of learning under the Druid's tutelage, even though she hadn't been promised such a situation. "Try to stop me," she'd said to Marius, narrowing her eyes. Marius had replied that he'd never even considered such an act.

In the corridor outside of Tahlia and Fara's room, Healer Albus whispered to them and Marius.

"They found runes charcoaled onto the floor in Ophelia's chambers. The Bloodworkers also determined that both the former commander's and Ophelia's blood were present on a knife found in the former commander's rooms as well as on the small rug that had covered the runes in Ophelia's apartments."

Tahlia wasn't surprised. But she had more questions. Rumors were zipping about the castle, and there were a lot of hushed mentions of a ritual book. "What book is everyone whispering about?"

"Yes," Albus said, "the dark magic book. Unseelie runes and so forth. A witness saw Ophelia take the book from the library. They asked to remain anonymous."

"Don't blame them," Fara mumbled.

Marius crossed his arms. Anger rolled off him, threads of the deepest orange shimmering from his body to lace around Tahlia like a protective barrier. "So Ophelia did indeed murder her father to do blood magic."

"I believe so," Albus said. "I don't think she knew exactly what she was doing though. At least to the extent of the evil she wrought. The Druid confirmed that when I met with him upon his arrival."

Fara grinned. "I love him so much."

Albus nodded at his new Healer student. "Talented male, for certain. We are blessed to have him in the Realm of Lights."

"What about Ophelia's admission to Tahlia about the poisoning? Any physical proof for the others?" Marius asked, brows knitted.

"We found two vials of ghostmint, one full and one empty, in Ophelia's bedchamber."

"I'd say I'm surprised about all of this," Tahlia said, "but I'd be lying."

All sets of eyes snapped to her face. Her human blood would never stop making her stick out a bit from the crowd at Dragon Tail Peak.

Marius let his arms fall and the threads around him faded into that ghostly transparency they normally had when Tahlia wasn't focusing on them and when the emotions of anyone nearby weren't running high.

"I knew it, too," Marius said. "And I apologize for not pressing the issue to Commander Gaius as soon as I guessed it."

"Stop apologizing for that," Tahlia said. "I forgave you already. Let's move on to what I'm actually annoyed with you about."

Marius raised an eyebrow and pursed his lips. "If you bring up the fact that I let you sleep through breakfast again…"

Fara stepped between Tahlia and Marius as Albus chuckled.

"You'll do what?" Fara asked, fists bunching.

Marius looked to the ceiling. "I will request an extra plate of crystal cakes for the both of you while you are preparing for the ceremony."

"One thing that is, um, less conducive to our more settled state of mind here…" Albus tilted his head and studied Tahlia.

"What is it?" she asked.

"The Druid can't help Lija."

The breath went out of Tahlia, and Marius took her

arm. If Lija never flew again, she would die. Tahlia knew it as surely as she knew her own name.

Albus continued, "Her wound has a strange lacing of dark magic. But he is wondering if the humans' Witch might be able to do something."

"Really?" Fara asked.

Tahlia chewed her lip. "Would she?"

Shrugging, Albus worried the edge of his cloak. "The Druid said he will ask."

"I can make a request of King Lysanael and Queen Revna myself," Marius said.

"Thank you," Tahlia said. "All of you."

They thanked Albus again for the information about Ophelia, and he left, wishing them well.

Fara linked her arm in Tahlia's. "Sorry, Commander Marius, but I need to steal your promised mate. It is time to fancy her up!"

The Witch would heal Lija. She had to.

Tahlia laughed with Fara and shook her head. "I'm already dreading what type of corsetry you have decided on."

Marius kissed Tahlia, his lips warm and firm. "My heart beats solely for our upcoming bonding."

Fara let out a dreamy sigh as Marius left the corridor. "He is still scary even though he's in love."

"More scary, really. You should have seen the protective threads humming around him while Albus was talking." Tahlia let out a breath, her shoulders finally relaxing. At last, they knew what Ophelia had done, they'd lived through it, and it was time to move forward.

"I wish I could see them. Do they look like wool?"

"Sort of."

They chitchatted happily and entered the bedchamber to prepare for the wedding.

"You look perfect," Maiwenn said as she finished cramming another mountain bluewing blossom into Tahlia's complicated braids. "You don't need more nature shoved into your hair. Not that anyone is asking me for beauty tips."

Fara shooed Maiwenn back and adjusted the blooms as well as the circlet of golden laurel leaves Tahlia wore. Fara's fingers were light and quick, unlike Maiwenn's. "They're the commander's favorite."

Maiwenn covered her mouth and her shoulders shook. "Commander Marius has a favorite flower?"

Fara whirled, glaring. "I know you can murder me with one move, but I will land at least one hit before death if you keep teasing them."

"Calm yourself, Lady Fara. I'll back off. I don't want you to stop making my evening tonic. That stuff works miracles." Maiwenn faced Tahlia. "Why are you so quiet?"

Tahlia's lips pulled into a wide grin. "I was just thinking about what Lija told me this morning."

All the riders could now speak with their dragons because Fara had made it her mission over the last fortnight to travel and retrieve an entire basket of *salvia scarletta*, the plant with blood-red leaves that connected the minds of dragons and their bonded riders.

"What did she say?" Maiwenn asked. "I'm still surprised Donan has a northern accent."

"I mean, he is a Seabreak," Fara said.

Maiwenn wrinkled her nose. "I'd thought most of them were born on the eastern coast."

It had to be odd to hear a very Northern pirate-type accent in one's head. "Lija said because Marius and I chose the crystals for our ritual that even dragons would respect our bond. That we have accidentally mimicked the old dragon ways."

Maiwenn's eyes widened. "Do they bond in a version of marriage too?"

"Many of them used to," Tahlia said, "but their traditions have changed over the centuries. It is seen as a very serious announcement of dedication now."

"Fitting, I think," Fara said. Then she glanced at the candle that marked the hours on the bronze shelf near the door. "Oh! We have to go now. You're going to be late! Commander Marius will think you're standing him up!"

"Everything is fine, Fara. Now, give me a solid hug, my old friend."

Fara leaned down and wrapped Tahlia in her spindly arms. "I love you. If you need me to strangle your mate at any point for not pleasing you, just let me know."

Maiwenn snorted. "I doubt you could complete that task, Healer. Also, is it odd being so aggressive and wanting to heal at the same time?"

"I don't feel both ways at the same time. Plus," Fara said with a slightly dangerous grin, "life and death go hand in hand."

"Aye, they do," Tahlia said. "But please don't murder anyone today, all right?"

Fara stepped back and began straightening up the vanity table. "It's up to everyone to behave properly," she said in a cheery voice.

Tahlia exchanged a glance with Maiwenn, who mouthed, *She's scary*.

Laughing, Tahlia stood and smoothed her blue-green skirts. The embroidered gold sigils—Tahlia's chosen dragon's tooth over an oak's silhouette—ran in stripes down the cascading folds of fabric. The sigils sparkled in the window's light. She wore a military-grade vest complete with draped mail and circles of bronze plating that hugged her shape. The capped and embroidered sleeves of a fine wool shirt peeked out at the shoulders. The outfit was exactly as she'd wanted it to be—reminiscent of the first riders' vests, but still having that feminine beauty to it in the voluminous skirts. And her Weaver's belt remained at her waist, the wool a bright red and humming with power.

Fara and Maiwenn rushed her out of the keep and down the narrow steps that led to the small mountain glen just beyond the courtyard. The wind from the cliff's edge swept over them, stirring fabric and Maiwenn's unbound hair. They hurried around the corner to find the other riders gathered alongside much of the castle staff, all the Healers—Fara's new associates—and most of the Bloodworkers. Titus lifted his hand in a quick wave, his eyes shining. Tahlia winked at him.

At the rocky outcropping that butted against the keep, a jagged array of crystals in purple, gold, clear, pink, and sage green sparkled. Lija, Ragewing, and several other dragons perched above, scales glittering in the setting sun.

Morning, friend, Tahlia said to Lija.

Happy bonding, rider.

Tahlia smiled up at Lija, pride swelling at the sight of the dragon that claimed a big piece of her heart.

The mottled light through the pines flitted across the crystals' varied surfaces as if in welcome. Courage, connection, and health energies flowed from the crystals. Before meeting Mother Twilight, Tahlia had only felt the crystals' power once—when a tremor in the earth had jostled the rose-hued ones and sparked the natural attraction between Marius and her. It had been intense. But now, as she watched the threads twinkle in and out of view, she recognized the hum of encouragement from the purple crystals especially. Perhaps the magic somehow knew she was nervous. She smiled and welcomed that energy in, stepping forward. Marius walked out of the shadows of the pines to join her at the crystals.

Head crowned with a golden laurel circlet like Tahlia's, Marius wore a draping dark blue cloak. His sigil showed on the bronze clasp at his throat—a partially coiled whip and a crystal cluster. A newly fashioned white leather military vest covered his broad chest and trim stomach. He wore riders' leather trousers as well as typical rider boots. He looked every inch the powerful Fae leader he was now. Commander of the Order of Mist Knights.

But more lovely than any of his raiment was the look

in Marius's eyes. Love shimmered from their gray depths and Tahlia couldn't wait to start her life with this male. Already she longed to whisk him away from the crowd and into their shared bedchamber. She wanted to trade whispers in the sunset light, feel his palms warming her belly and thighs, listen to his sighs of happiness and contentment...

"Your beauty is beyond any phrase I could utter, my lady," he whispered in his deep and melodious voice. The breeze stirred his hair and ruffled his cloak.

Joy danced inside her. They had made it.

The ceremony went as planned. First, they burned a beeswax and sage candle for Gaius, asking those attending for a moment of quiet in respect. Then, together, Tahlia and Marius burned dragon lavender at the base of the crystals and detailed their gratitude for their dragons and for the mountains that housed them. Touching a fist to their temples each, they sealed their offering of herbs.

Next, they set their palms against the rose-colored crystal, and Healer Albus wrapped their hands in the braided handfasting cord. The old male spoke the holy words, and once Tahlia and Marius laced their fingers, faced each cardinal direction, and voiced their intent to mate, their bond was formed. Marius's hands were so warm and comforting. Tahlia never wanted to let go.

With a rush of light, threads leapt around their joined hands. The ties of energy sparkled and undulated like waves on the sea.

"What is it?" Marius looked down at her, wonder in his gaze.

"The threads... We are united in deep blue and gold threads of energy. It's amazing."

"You are amazing, my love, my mate."

They kissed chastely, and the crowd cheered as they swept past the gathering and headed back to the keep for the feast.

CHAPTER 36
TAHLIA

The chambers that had once been Marius's alone now belonged to them both, allowing Fara to remain in the room in the riders' wing on her own as she worked toward becoming a Healer. Off the main living area, a balcony overlooked the pine forest to the west and the peaks that flanked Dragon Tail.

Stars lit the sky and Tahlia leaned back against Marius's chest as they finished their bottle of wine. Tahlia's stomach tangled into knots. She was glad she hadn't eaten too much during the feasting and games that had run all day after the ceremony.

Marius took her empty cup. "What's troubling you, my perfect mate?"

He set his and hers on the small round table beside the railing before turning and pulling her close. His scent of cloves and stormy skies enveloped her as surely as his arms.

"Honestly? I'm nervous." A laugh escaped her. She felt whole and loved with him, but this was an entirely new level of attachment. "I'm worried you'll come to regret asking me to be your mate." Her cheeks went hot and she shook her head at herself for being silly.

He hugged her tightly and pressed his lips to the top of her head. He was just so very tall. "I'm anxious too, love."

"You are?"

"Of course. We both want this night to be special. It's more than simply having some fun."

That was true. She did feel that pressure to make this night wonderful in every way.

"Plus," he continued, "we have made the most serious commitment possible, outside of our vows to the order. Neither one of us is being flippant about our relationship. That gives this night a certain gravity."

Smiling into his chest, she toyed with the edges of his vest. He was right about all of it. "But we have a lifetime of nights spread out before us."

"Exactly. So we need not put too much pressure on this evening. In fact," he said, pulling away to look into her eyes, "if you would rather wait to consummate our bond, I can—"

"No, no, no." She curled her hands over his shoulders, then stood on tiptoe to kiss the underside of his jaw.

He hummed in appreciation. "Whatever pleases you, I will do it. Just say the word. Give the order."

She let her head fall back and he took the hint to kiss his way down her throat. Warmth shot down her body, coiling low. His fingers dug into her hips, a delightfully rough grip that sent her blood racing through her veins. While one hand slid low to ruck up her skirts, his lips claimed hers in a kiss that was in no way gentle but insistent instead. His hand found the warmth beneath her skirts, and she gasped. Letting out another hum of approval, Marius kneaded her with his knuckles. Bolts of pleasure branched through her like lightning.

A growl rumbled from his chest into hers and she linked her arms around his neck. He lifted her and carried her to the bedchamber off the living area. A fire crackled and snapped in the bedroom's hearth and shadows rippled across the curtains draping the bed. Standing beside the bed, they tugged off their leathers, then took turns undressing one another, a layer at a time.

Once they were stripped bare, he laid her on the voluminous blankets and pillows. He crawled on top of her and drew his lips across her cheek and forehead. His body pressed against hers. She peered down between them as he nibbled the sensitive tip of her ear. His stomach muscles pulled tight and the sight of him fully bared to her in all his masculine beauty had her gasping. Heat rose between her thighs. He moved down her body, mouth grazing her breasts, navel, and hips as he traveled.

"You're exquisite, stunning, completely and utterly breathtaking," he whispered over her skin, his breath tickling and teasing.

She couldn't do anything more than moan and twist her fingers in his long hair.

With slow flicks of his tongue, he stroked her center until she was trembling. He spread his hands over her lower stomach to hold her in place, and she writhed, unable to remain still. Delight shivered inside her, ready to unfurl.

"Marius, please."

"Yes?"

"I want you. Here," she said, tugging handfuls of his hair.

He chuckled, the sound deep and gravelly. In a rush of movement, he lay on top of her again, his body poised perfectly. Impatience had her bucking against his cock. The feel of his heat on hers was unlike anything else in the world. She latched onto his shoulders and tried to urge him to enter, but he held back, grinning like a dragon about to blaze an enemy.

With one hand, he took hold of both her wrists. He pinned them on the smooth wood of the headboard and began to roll his hips, still refusing to give her what she truly wanted. She let out a groan, the desire overcoming any nervous feeling left inside her. She needed him. Now.

"Marius. Take me. Stop torturing me."

"I think you quite like this punishment."

Pleasure scattered across her torso, peaking her breasts, then traveling down the backs of her legs to pebble her skin in waves.

Two could play this game. She bit her lip, stared into his eyes, and wrapped her legs around him in one swift maneuver.

His lips parted in a gasp and he winced, hissing, his fangs showing and the veins in his neck growing prominent.

"Be still," he growled, going still himself as well.

She grinned. "Why?" She rocked herself against the length of him.

Snarling, he suddenly dropped his hips and thrust into her. He drove forward again and again and again.

"You are mine, Tahlia." His voice was the storm-tossed forest. "Mine. All mine."

The bed shook beneath the fervor of his pace, and pure pleasure whipped through her body, the heat inside her unfurling and snapping, making her cry out.

Dropping to the bed, he wrapped his arms around her and tucked her up beside him. Sweat made their skin stick here and there, but everything was perfection because this love was real and it was forever.

EPILOGUE
MARIUS

In the months that followed, Marius was never satisfied when it came to showing Tahlia love. In word and in deed, both in the bedchamber and outside those walls, he did his best to honor the love of his life, his dear and perfect mate.

And it wasn't just because a certain female Healer would stab him repeatedly if he did anything less. Fara actually seemed to like him now. Perhaps even trust him.

It was because Tahlia deserved to be treated like a goddess, and he'd be damned if he didn't make up for all the trouble he'd caused early on by not acting on his heart's knowledge from day one.

Remus is concerned, Ragewing said into Marius's mind. *He smells of fear.*

Is it Lija? Tahlia's dragon still hadn't healed well enough to fly and the Witch hadn't yet responded to their pleas for assistance.

No. Something else.

The squire rounded the corner and entered Ragewing's stall. He held out a sealed letter. "This came for you. From one of the king's messengers."

Marius set aside the cloth he'd been using to polish Ragewing's shoulder scales and accepted the letter. "What's wrong, Remus?"

"The male, he..." Remus rubbed at his nose and glanced away.

The seal bore Fae King Lysanael's seal. Marius cracked it and opened the missive.

Remus met Marius's gaze. "The messenger's horse died shortly after arriving. He rode him too hard because this message is so urgent."

"Why didn't the queen ride her forest dragon here, I wonder..."

"There's word she is in Fjordbok at the moment."

The queen's home. "Ah." Marius scanned the letter, his heart dropping with each new detail. "Remus, find Tahlia for me, will you?"

"No need," a quick and perfect voice said from the stall doorway. Tahlia lifted a hand in greeting.

A wave of concern swept over Marius and he had to restrain himself from pulling her to him protectively. He swallowed and met her at the door.

"King Lysanael and Queen Revna have set us on a mission."

"Oooh." She rubbed her hands together. "Will Ragewing let me ride with you since Lija is still healing?"

Marius could tell Tahlia was ignoring the potentially lethal elements of Lija's condition. Dragons that didn't fly, didn't stay alive for long. But for now, that issue had to wait.

"This is no standard set of instructions, Lady Tahlia. Only you and I are ordered to meet with the king. It is a secret mission and highly dangerous."

She bit her lip and looked up at him. "Order me as you see fit, Commander Marius."

"I'm serious."

"Oh, I know." She wiggled her eyebrows.

Desire and frustration warred inside Marius. He wanted to take her into his arms... He gritted his teeth and forcibly cleared his mind of those wayward emotions.

"This mission involves the most powerful artifact in history. An evil human, some type of lesser king, has somehow gained the artifact in question."

"If we are headed to the human kingdom, we can talk to the Witch about Lija ourselves!"

"Possibly, yes. Especially if our king and queen approve, which they should."

"What else?" she asked, courage practically beaming from her eyes like rainbows.

As concerned as he was, he still couldn't help but delight in how wonderful she was.

"We are to infiltrate the human kingdom during something deemed a *tomato festival*. There will be costumes and a parade," he said, shuddering.

A laugh snapped from Tahlia's smiling mouth. "I'll risk anything to see you dressed up like a vegetable. Or is it technically a fruit? When do we leave?"

Marius pinched the bridge of his nose and hoped they weren't about to die after all the work they'd put into staying alive.

. . .

READERS,

THANK you so much for joining Tahlia, Marius, and the rest of the *Bound by Dragons* crew for another adventure. I hope you'll order *Crown and Dragon*, Book Three! (should be out Fall 2024)

FOR ALL THE *Bound by Dragons* bonus materials (extra art, maps, character interviews, etc.), join my newsletter here: https://www.alishaklapheke.com/free-prequel-1

THANKS FOR MAKING my stories possible!
    Alisha

Also by Alisha Klapheke

Realm of Dragons and Fae Series (same world as Bound by Dragons)

Kingdoms of Lore Series

Dragons Rising Series Omnibus

And many more...

See all the books at alishaklapheke.com

Printed in Great Britain
by Amazon